SO-BAV-604

MAXIMUM INSECURITY

MAXIMUM INSECURITY

BY
P. J. GRADY

For Renée,
A new friend of mine, an
old friend of my dear
Penny's
PJ

MEMENTO MORI MYSTERY

A Memento Mori Mystery
Published by
Avocet Press Inc
635 Madison Avenue, Suite 400
New York, NY 10022
http://www.avocetpress.com

AVOCET PRESS

Copyright © 1999 by P. J. Grady

All rights reserved. No part of this book may be reproduced or transmitted
in any form or by any means, electronic or mechanical, including photocopy-
ing, recording, or by any information storage and retrieval system, without
written permission from the author, except for the inclusion of brief quota-
tions in review.

Library of Congress Cataloging-in-Publication Data

Grady, P. J.
    Maximum Insecurity / by P. J. Grady.
    p. cm. — (Memento mori mystery)
  ISBN 0-9661072-4-1
  I. Mexican Americans — New Mexico — Fiction. I. Title
  II. Series.
PS3557.R1235M39   1999
813´ .54 — dc21   98-52320
                                             CIP

Cover photographs copyright © 1999 Susan Hazen-Hammond
Permission granted by the Santa Fe County Detention Center

Printed in the USA
First Edition

To
Kathrin Kinzer-Ellington
and
Tony Sawtell

Justice, justice thou shalt pursue.
Deut. 16:20

Author's Note:

I've peopled the ancient city of Santa Fe with the figments of my own imagination. Any resemblance to the living (or the dead) is entirely coincidental. Any resemblance between the Spanish (or "Splanglish") spoken in northern New Mexico and the Spanish spoken elsewhere is astounding.

Dime con quien andas y te diré quien eres.

Tell me who you hang with, and
I'll tell you who you are.

CHAPTER ONE

At the Texas State Prison, you can put out a contract on a man's life for a cupcake. At the Penitentiary of New Mexico, it'll cost you at least a carton of cigarettes.

Most inmates at the penitentiary smoke. The canteen's only open one day a week, but it does a bang-up business in coffin nails.

Inmate Isaac "Gordo" Gonzáles didn't smoke. Gordo didn't believe in polluting the temple of your body with tobacco, alcohol or illegal drugs. You get a headache, you take an aspirin. That's okay. Sex is okay, too. Sex is natural. When the Lord commanded Adam and Eve to "be fruitful and multiply," He wasn't talking test tube babies. In the closed world of the pen, La Pinta, sex is hard to come by, but Gordo had an angle. Sure. Cons like Gordo know all the angles.

Every day, Gordo worked out in the gym at the South Facility, pumping iron. It was something to do, like art class or hobby shop or hanging with the homies in the yard. But pumping iron is a wise investment of a man's time. The hours spent in the gym could save his life.

Gordo had heard about the riot which engulfed the pen in 1980. All the cons know about it the way you know about AIDS or pepperoni pizza. You don't remember who told you, but you know about it anyway. Nobody knows how many inmates died. The records burned when rioters torched the Main Facility. Nobody mourns the nameless dead, but their spirits haunt the ruined cell blocks in the Main to this day.

Gordo Gonzáles was afraid of ghosts, but he wasn't afraid of any man alive, not even Sweet Papa Foster. Any man with more smarts than Gordo would have had the sense to be afraid of Foster, but, by working out, Gordo figured he could build himself up to handle anything. Everybody said it was only a matter of time before La Pinta erupted again into fire and blood. Gordo was a big man, and he kept in shape. If trouble came, he reckoned he could handle it.

On a warm September afternoon, Gordo strolled into the gym. Most of the guys were out in the yard, watching a softball game. The sky above the Cerrillos Hills was as blue as the Virgin's mantle, trimmed with cumulus clouds. It would rain in a couple of hours, but by then the institution would be in lockdown. It was a shame to be in lockdown on such a beautiful day. It was too beautiful a day to die.

A couple of kids were working out on the far side of the gym. Gordo didn't know them. He figured they were *pachucos*, gang members, maybe, or wannabees. Lots of *'chucos* coming into La Pinta lately. Gordo shook his head sadly. It wasn't the same no more. These kids, they don't got no respect. They don't understand the way things gotta be. One of the *'chucos* had his shirt off, revealing a torso covered by tattoos. On his back, the Virgin of Guadalupe opened her arms to shower roses on the heads of a biker and his naked lady.

Buckets was in the gym, too, but nobody paid any attention to Buckets. Nobody ever paid him any mind. Looking for cigarette butts, Buckets rummaged through the trash as always. He hummed a little tune as usual, the same bars over and over. "De dum dum dum diddle dum."

But there was no CO anywhere in the gym.

That should have set off alarms in Gordo's head. A corrections officer is posted to the gym whenever it's open to inmates. It's his job to watch them at play, like a kindergarten teacher at recess. He doesn't

10

eat on the job or drink a cup of coffee or read the funnies. He doesn't chew the fat with the fellas. He doesn't leave his post for any reason, not even to go to the john.

But Gordo didn't know there was no CO.

He set the weights in place and lay on his back on the bench. Stretching his arms, he began to press: down, up, down, up. He was settling into an easy rhythm when the *'chucos* came over. Gordo ignored them. The one with the tattoos grinned at the other one, and they grabbed the bar, shoving it onto Gordo's chest and arms.

Like a beetle pinned to a board, Gordo couldn't move.

The next to the last thing Gordo ever saw was the cross tattooed on the *'chuco's* wrist. The last thing Gordo saw was Sweet Papa's coal-black face as Foster crashed a five-pound weight into Gordo's head.

Foster stuffed his bloody shirt into a trash can. Hard on the heels of the *pachucos*, he slipped out the door to join the crowd at the ballfield where Devere was thrown out trying to steal second. At the three-two pitch, Harrison flied out to the shortstop, stranding Aguilar on third.

Alone with the dead, Buckets hummed to himself.

Every week or so, Matty Madrid drove down Highway 14 to visit an old boyfriend at the pen. She didn't know why. After all, Mingo had walked out of her life ten years ago. She wouldn't let him in again if he were standing at the front door, his hat in his hand. Come to think of it, Mingo never wore a hat. But Matty knew that when you wall up a part of your heart, the walls themselves remind you what's inside.

"Yo, Mingo, how's it going?"

"Hiya, babe." Mingo grinned at her. He'd lost a button on his shirt. Medium and maximum security inmates wear identical uniforms, green workshirts and dark green denims. Minimums wear blue shirts and jeans like half the working stiffs in town. Matty wondered if the concerned citizens of Santa Fe know just how many work crews picking up trash along the highway are Penitentiary of New Mexico inmates.

Her grandfather's cousin, Cipi Vigil, had told her that when he moved to Santa Fe after the war, the old Territorial Prison on Pen Road was still in use. The convicts, as inmates were called in those days, wore stripes with numbers stenciled on the back.

Today, in their greens at La Pinta, inmates wear no numbers, no nameplates, although staff is required to wear picture ID at all times. Makes you wonder who's keeping tabs on who, Matty sometimes thought.

"Hey," Mingo said, "I heard about the job you did catchin' that fuckin' baby raper. Little piece of shit!"

"Yeah, I figured they were gonna send him up here from RDC."

"Not here, leastways, not at South. He gets outta the fish tank, RDC, you know, they send him over to North. They got all the fuckin' PC's there. Baby rapers, hey, they're all PC's. Guys find out about 'em, they sure as hell beat the crap out of 'em."

The pen's North Facility is about a mile away from the South Facility as the crow flies. There are no crows at La Pinta, but there are flocks of ravens, feeding on the refuse of overflowing garbage containers, nourished by the atmosphere of death and decay. The North Facility houses maximum security inmates, protective custody or PC's, administrative and disciplinary segregation, and death row. The death house itself doubles as the property office at North. After all, nobody has been executed in the Land of Enchantment since 1960.

Mingo shifted uncomfortably in his chair. "Got a job for you, babe."

"*You* do? Mingo…"

"Okay, it ain't for me. Like, it's for this dude I know."

"So, have him call me. I'll accept the charges."

Mingo chuckled. "Hafta be long distance, babe. Awful long. Yeah. Dude's roastin' in hell by now, I figger." He suddenly sobered. "Maybe hell ain't so far away from La Pinta."

"Mingo, what're you talking about?"

"Okay, okay. Dude name of Isaac Gonzáles got hisself wasted here a while back."

"Isaac... Gordo Gonzáles. Yeah, I read about it. But, hey, the paper said it was an accident."

"Yeah, well, don't believe everything you read in the papers. They're gonna print the bullshit Corrections give 'em. Half the time the department don't even know what's happenin'. They jes' git told what to say, an' they say it."

"Slow down, slow down. Tell me what happened."

"Okay. See, babe, they found old Gordo dead in the gym. He'd been bench pressin', see, and he was layin' on the bench, flat on his back, and this weight squished in his goddam head."

"Anybody see what happened?"

"Nah, there wasn't no CO or nothin', only Buckets, and he don't count."

"Howzat?" Matty asked.

"You dunno Buckets. He's a reg'lar full-mooner. Dunno what planet he's at half the time. Anyhow, Investigations investigated and says it was a accident owing to as a result of Gordo, he got real careless."

"And the State Police? The OMI? What do they say?"

"Corrections didn't call 'em in. It was a accident. 'Member?"

"Okay, so..."

"So, the family wants to sue. They wanna take Corrections to the cleaners or, like, the company that made the bench or somebody, anybody. I said maybe you'd look into it for 'em."

"What are you, my agent?"

Mingo just laughed.

"Yeah, okay, I'll look into it." Matty nodded. "But I don't know

I'll find anything. I can't even get into the gym to look around."

"Sure, you can. Yard event's comin' up on Saturday. I can show you the gym. You talk to Buckets. Hell, that'll be a trip, awright."

"Hey, a yard event. I've never been to one of those."

"Outta Joint at the Joint, real *chiribí*. Live music and barbeque, dudes' kids, their wives, shit, even their girlfriends. Hell of a time."

"Okay. In the meantime, I'll talk to Gordo's folks. You got the address?" Mingo said she'd find Gordo's mother in Goose Neck, a village near the town of Las Vegas, New Mexico, about an hour's drive from Santa Fe. "You tell 'em my fees? Fifty dollars a day plus expenses."

Mingo wriggled uncomfortably. "I kinda, like, told 'em you could do it on, like, a contingency basis."

"Contingency? Shit! What makes you think I'd work for a contingency fee? No way, Mingo! Fifty dollars a day plus expenses, and I want a retainer, too, $250, before I do a damn thing."

"They ain't got it, babe. They're poor people, ain't hardly gettin' by. His mom's a old lady. His brother got bunged up somethin' terrible, and he's on disability. They need your help, Matt."

Matty looked at Mingo. "What's in it for you?"

"Me?"

"Yeah, you. What's in it for you, bro? And don't gimme any crap about loving your fellow man. You're no more of a saint than I am."

"Hey, you're right about that, for sure." There was a longish pause. "Okay, yeah. I got 'em to agree to pay me a contingency fee, too. But, hey, only if they win. They lose, they don't owe me nothin'."

"What if they win and they don't pay you?"

Mingo shrugged. "I got friends in Albuquerque break both their legs."

"Oh, for chriss… who's their lawyer? They got a lawyer?"

"No, well, I was, like, kinda thinkin' you might talk to your old friend Rodney…"

"No way, José! Kleiner, Sprague and Stone is a real heavy hitter. You think they'd represent the family of some con who dropped a dumbbell …"

"Weight."

"… on his *cabeza*? That's the dumbest…"

"Hey, you don't ask, you don't know. Do it for me, babe. *¿En tenga?*"

Matty didn't wait until she got home to call Rodney Stone. About a mile from La Pinta, she pulled into Allsup's. Sipping a Slush Puppie, she dialed Kleiner, Sprague and Stone. Better get this over with, she thought. Rodney Stone was an old friend from Santa Fe High, but he didn't owe her any favors. She figured he'd say no.

She was right. "Sweetie, not little Rodney's cup of Lapsang at all."

"I know, Rod. Sorry to bother you."

"But…"

"But? What do you mean, 'but'?"

"It just so happens a friend of mine…"

She groaned.

"Nothing like that, ducky bumps. I've known Dodi's family for years. She's just been admitted to the bar, and…"

"*She?*"

"She's a she. Didn't I say? She's decided to go solo instead of joining a firm or enlisting under the PD's banner of 'truth, justice, and the American way.' She could use the business."

"Contingency fee?"

"Talk to her. Dodi Koren. She's on San Francisco Street, upstairs over the Reimann Gallery. I don't think she has a phone yet. They promised her one *mañana,* but that was three weeks ago. I'll give information a jingle."

"Yeah, right." But Matty sympathized with Dodi's problems with the phone company. In Santa Fe, Ma Bell's "tomorrow" means only "not today."

Matty climbed the stairs to Dodi Koren's office. A petite brunette in a miniskirt was at the file cabinet, her back to the door.

"'Scuse me. I'm looking for Ms. Koren? Dodi Koren?"

"I'm Dodi Koren," the woman said, turning around. "What can I do for you?"

"My name's Matty Madrid, and I'm…"

"Oh, right! Rodney called. I didn't expect you so soon. Come on in, and we'll talk."

Dodi's office was about the size of a walk-in closet in suburbia. Matty slipped onto a ladder-back chair opposite the attorney.

"So, you got your phone," she said.

Dodi grimaced. "I've got a phone, okay. They gave me the number of a contractor who just went out of business. Phone's been ringing off the hook. Irate customers up the kazoo."

"Too bad."

"Not really. Half of them want to sue. So, what have we got?"

"Nothing yet." Matty made a face. "I just wanted to touch base with you before I talk to the family, see if they got a case."

"Fill me in."

"Isaac 'Gordo' Gonzáles was an inmate at the state pen. He was lifting weights, bench-pressing, and one of them slipped and crushed his skull."

"Hold it! I know something about pumping iron. My second husband was a power-lifter. Real health nut. You know the type. Wouldn't eat any chocolate. Had to be carob." She shuddered. "Granola every morning. Massive coronary at the age of thirty-seven."

"Jeez! I didn't know. I'm sorry."

"It's okay. We were divorced. Twice. What I'm saying is you couldn't drop the damn thing on your head, even if you tried to."

"Hey, I dunno from nothing. So far my info comes from an inmate, and he wasn't even there."

"It's pretty flimsy, Matty. Okay I call you Matty?"

"¡No problema, Dodi! So, what if it happened like they say?"

"We'd have to prove negligence, get a good look at the apparatus, maybe sound out some witnesses if we're going to put together a case against Corrections."

"There weren't any witnesses. Nobody saw it happen."

"No, I mean, people who'd used the bench before, somebody who noticed it wasn't kosher. Maybe a guard reported a problem. Nice little paper trail would be a big help."

Matty sighed. "I don't think it's possible. Those *pendejos* in Corrections cover their backsides pretty good. That weight bench is probably at a county landfill by now."

"Well, you can tell the family we might—*might*—have a case under the Tort Claims Act if we can prove negligence."

"Negligence?"

"'Negligent operation of a building.' Like I say, we'd have to prove it. It's going to take a little work."

"'Kay, 'negligent operation of a building,' huh? Yeah, I had a case like that." She frowned, trying to remember. "It'll come to me. So, general all-around dumbness doesn't count?"

"Not in law." Dodi grinned. "You want to triple the number of tort claims filed? No, you're up against the doctrine of sovereign immunity. 'The king can do no wrong.'"

"The hell he can't!"

"Well, the point is there are only a handful of things for which you can sue the state. 'Negligent operation of a building' is one of them. Sounds like what we have here, wrongful death resulting from negligence. It's worth a try."

"Is there such a thing as rightful death?" Matty asked as she got up to go.

"What's more, in March of '94 the state supreme court allowed claims for loss of consortium. That's a first for New Mexico."

"Con...sounds like high finance."

"Consortium." Dodi smiled. "The loss of a loved one's companionship."

It was Matty's turn to smile. "From what I know about Gordo, I figure Mrs. Gonzáles owes the state for the loss of his companionship and not the other way around."

Dodi looked at her watch and frowned. "I'm due in court," she said. "I'm representing a client who was cited for not wearing his seat belt."

"Not wearing his seat belt? That's only a misdemeanor. What does he need a lawyer for?"

"It's a civil complaint. My client's the plaintiff. Claims the seat belt law's a violation of the ADA."

"ADA?"

"Americans with Disabilities Act. My client's claustrophobic. Buckling up exacerbates his condition. Hey, Matty, I want to be sure you understand. At the moment, it's not my case, and I wouldn't be able to afford an investigator anyway. But I'll be happy to talk to the family."

"Yeah, well, wish I could say the same."

Matty took I-25 to Goose Neck. At a "goose neck," a bend in the river, the town of Los Sumideros slumbered beside the Pecos until, in 1889, an Anglo postmaster changed its name from Sumideros to something he could spell. The post office closed in 1936, but the name, "Goose Neck," remained. Sometimes the locals called it "Goose Neck" and sometimes "Sumideros," but it didn't matter. They knew exactly what they meant.

She stopped by a cluster of trailers to ask directions. A small boy with a dirty face scooped up a handful of mud and threw it against the side of Matty's truck.

"¡*Ya chole*!" She shouted as she gunned the engine and drove away.

At Bevo's, the bartender directed her to the Gonzáles house, a two-room adobe in need of a new coat of plaster. Adobes are replastered every year by the women of the family or by the village plasterer, the *zoquetera*. But it looked like Goose Neck's *zoquetera* had followed the postmaster into history.

A couple of scrawny chickens scratching in the yard was the only sign of industry. Matty didn't think anybody was at home until the screen door suddenly flew open and a man came hurtling out. He carried a Winchester 75, and he pointed the business end at Matty's heart.

"Oh, shit!" she said.

Half turning, the rifleman hollered into the house. "Momma!" He continued to level the .22 at his target as he shuffled to one side, making room on the porch for his mother.

Momma was the largest woman Matty had ever seen, maybe three hundred fifty, maybe four hundred pounds. She wore a flowered shift and terrycloth slippers. When she spoke, her voice was as harsh as a scrub jay's.

"Yeah?"

"Mrs. Gonzáles? Listen, I'm Matty Madrid. I'm a private investigator, and I'm here about the death of your son."

"Momma!" The man with the Winchester seemed alarmed.

"Shaddup, Sonny. She means Ikie. Put that bunny blammer down 'fore you shoot another hole in the roof again." He lowered the rifle obediently. "Git on in here." It took Matty a moment to realize Mrs. Gonzáles was addressing her.

Matty was on unfamiliar ground. She'd expected to find herself in a traditional Spanish-speaking household, a careworn *vieja* clutching a rosary to her withered breast.

But Mrs. Gonzáles and her son conversed in English, in the nasal twang of the Ozark highlands. It didn't take a detective to deduce Mrs. Gonzáles was an Anglo who had married a Hispanic and settled into domestic bliss beside the Pecos. Matty wondered what had happened to Mr. Gonzáles. Wherever he was, he probably didn't have call-forwarding.

Mrs. Gonzáles sat down heavily in a rump-sprung easy chair. Neither she nor her son moved to turn off the television set. Once again, the Roadrunner outwitted Wiley Coyote. Matty sat on the edge of the couch and Sonny sat down beside her, so close their thighs touched. It was time to establish a few ground rules.

"Back off, bro, or I stick your ugly nose up your ass." The matriarch of the family grinned, displaying broken yellow teeth. Fiddling with the pink bandanna he wore about his head like a *pachuco,* Sonny scooted away from Matty. Mingo had said Gordo's brother was disabled. She'd expected somebody in a wheelchair, a vet, maybe, or the victim of a drunk driver, the scourge of New Mexico's highways. She hadn't realized Sonny was two tacos short of a combination plate.

"Okay, Mrs. Gonzáles, let's talk turkey," Matty said. "Darryl Mínguez told me what happened to your son…"

"Mingo!" Sonny began bouncing up and down.

"Yeah, Mingo. He said you were thinking about suing the state. I talked to this lawyer…" Matty handed Dodi's card to the old lady. "Maybe you can sue, maybe not. It'll take an investigation to determine whether you gotta case."

"Investigation. An' that's you, huh?"

"That's me. I'll need a retainer plus fifty dollars a day and expenses."

Mrs. Gonzáles guffawed. Sonny giggled, following his momma's lead. For a slow learner, he picked up some things mighty fast.

Matty got up to go. "I'm gonna give you my card, too. You think about it. Okay?"

Matty hit the blacktop at eighty, anxious to leave the adobe house and the Gonzáleses behind her. She'd gone eyeball-to-eyeball with a Mafia don and his "soldiers" once. Not even the godfather of the Front Range left as sour a taste in her mouth as Mother Gonzáles. She figured she'd seen the last of Goose Neck and its denizens for a while. If the old lady wouldn't pay her retainer, Matty wouldn't take the case. Some things you don't lose any sleep over.

In the tumbledown adobe, Mrs. Gonzáles turned to her surviving son. "G'wan, git me a beer," she said.

"We ain't got no beer, Momma." Sonny started to shake. He didn't like to say no to Momma, but they were clean out of beer. He'd had the last one himself for breakfast with a mess of sardines and crackers.

"I know that, hardhead! Git on down to Bevo's and git me some. Well, what're you waitin' fer?"

Sonny scurried out of the house. For a big man, he could move quickly. He carried the Winchester cradled in his arms like a baby. It was almost a part of him, and he took it everywhere. It's legal to carry a loaded weapon in New Mexico so long as it's not concealed, but it's illegal to take it into a bar. Max Gonzáles, the proprietor of Bevo's, knew that if he were to insist on a rigid enforcement of the gun laws, he'd lose most of his customers. You might as well try to stop them pissing in the Pecos.

Max was a distant cousin of Sonny, too distant to trace their common lineage. Because the locals tend to intermarry, there are a lot of Gonzáleses in Goose Neck. By marrying an Anglo, Sonny's father had demonstrated an uncommonly independent streak. Unfortunately, his marriage seemed to have done little to invigorate the stagnant gene pool.

"Gimme a beer, Max," Sonny said. "I gotta git Momma a beer."

"Sure, bro, sure. What you want?"

"Gimme a Coors. Momma likes Coors."

"Sure. How many of 'em you want?"

Momma hadn't told Sonny what to say. "Jes' one, I s'pose, Max. Momma don't want no more. Jes' gimme one."

"That'll be a buck fifty, bro."

But Sonny was broke. His wallet was as flat as a roadkill on the interstate. He'd spent the last of his money whoring in town Saturday night, and he didn't even have $1.50. On top of that, the whore hadn't been very nice to him. She'd hurt his feelings when she wouldn't let him do it bottoms up. He'd have been better off if he'd grabbed some girl off the street like the last time. At least she'd have put up a fight. Sonny liked it when they fought. It got him all excited. But he showed her. He showed the whore. When he punched her in the face, it felt really good, and then he had to do it to her again, but she didn't charge him the second time.

Sonny began to get excited just thinking about it until he remembered his empty wallet. Desire deflated in him like a flat tire. Momma sent him to get a beer. If he went home without it, Momma'd get mad.

That scared Sonny. Thinking about Momma scared him. It scared him to think that she'd get mad. It scared him so bad he soiled his pants.

"Oh, for God's sake…" Max gave him the beer just to get rid of him. One of his customers laughed. The tall, skinny man on the stool beside him didn't crack a smile. He nursed a cup of cold coffee between two pale hands.

Wearing a loopy grin, Sonny went home. By the time he reached the house, he'd forgotten all about changing his pants.

Anita was waiting for Matty at the front door. Anita was Matty's cousin, once removed, Cipi's daughter-in-law. Cipi and Manuel Madrid, Matty's grandfather, were first cousins, *primos,* and the best of friends. After Pearl Harbor, they'd enlisted together in the Coast Artillery. With nine hundred buddies, Manny Madrid died on Bataan, but cousin Cipi continued to look out for Manny's family. So, it was only natural that his daughter-in-law would be there when Matty needed her. Anita's heart was as big as Santa Fe Baldy.

Anita beamed. "Oh, Matty, I'm so glad you're here. Your grandmother, she's been having a real good day, only I gotta go home. Little

Frances Ann's been coughing and Tina's gonna take her to the doctor. I gotta go home and start the supper."

"Sure, but, 'Nita, I'm sorry the baby's sick."

"Oh, it's just a bug. You know. The babies get 'em all the time, only Tina, it's her first baby." She shrugged.

Matty smiled. "Hey, listen, you go on home. We'll be right as rain."

Anita hurried next door. For a moment, Matty remained in the doorway, thinking about her own little girl. When Esperanza was a baby, Matty's heart had missed a beat with every childish cough, every sneeze and sniffle.

She turned and walked into the house. Gran met her in the hallway. "You home, *jita*? I fix you something to eat." The good days, as 'Nita called them, were coming far between as Alzheimer's took its inevitable toll. You learned to treasure them, like happy memories of little Esperanza, squirreling them away to feed you in the long winter of the soul.

Gran went to bed early, but Matty sat up late. Sometimes when she wrestled with a problem, she'd talk it over with our Lady of Solitude, an image of the Blessed Virgin flanked by faded photographs of John XXIII and RFK. Matty, who hadn't been to confession since Esperanza's accident, didn't really believe Our Lady listened to what she had to say. But somehow it helped to talk things over with somebody who wouldn't argue or interrupt, somebody who was just there.

Matty found herself thinking of Erlene Gonzáles. One son in the pen and another one… She thought of Esperanza. *Who's to say Mrs. Gonzáles doesn't grieve for her lost child as I do for mine?*

The phone rang. Matty half expected to hear Mrs. Gonzáles's voice.

"Matty? Dodi Koren."

"Oh, hey, Dodi. I saw Mrs. Gonzáles…"

"I know. She called me. She wants to go full tilt on the lawsuit."

"*¡Bueno!* But I gotta tell you I don't think she's got any money."

23

Dodi chuckled. "I know. She called me collect from a bar in Goose Neck. I told her I'd take it on a contingency basis. That's okay, but I said I don't know about your fee."

"If she pays my retainer, $250, I'll bill her for services, Dodi. I gotta helluva collection agency. You know Dwight Anaya?"

"Popo, the Mexican Man Mountain? Sure, I saw him wrestle the Human Anaconda a couple of months ago. He's got a helluva sleeper. Put that sucker out so fast! God, I wouldn't want him after me."

"He's sweet, but he's kinda persistent, sorta like wasps in the jelly jar."

"I'll bet." Dodi cleared her throat. "Listen, Matty, there's something else…"

"There's always something else. What's up, Dodi?"

"I want you to find somebody for me."

"For a client?"

"No, for me. It's my husband, my third husband. I want you to find him."

"Your *third* husband?" Matty stared at the receiver. "Okay, what's the deal?"

"Herbie ducked out on me while we were living in Albuquerque. I was in law school at UNM, and he was in and out of the bars on Central."

"So? You don't need to find him to dump him."

"I don't care about the schlump, but I want my assets back. He cleaned out our checking account, our savings, some bonds my dad gave us, even my grandmother's diamond ring."

"Herbie… what? Koren?"

"Herbert Chass Koren. Five feet nine, one hundred sixty pounds, blond, balding, but he parts it on the side and tries to hide it. Born Shaker Heights, Ohio, December 11, 1961."

"What does he do for a living?"

"I told you, he's in and out of bars."

"I thought you meant he's a lush."

"Close. He's a comedian. Thinks he's gonna make it on Letterman someday."

"*¡Oh, chiste!* Hey, I'll see what I can do."

"Super. I'll tell Mrs. Gonzáles it's a go, so long as she comes up with your retainer. Oh, and, uh, I'll send you a retainer for finding Herbie. Cross my heart. Okay?"

"*Bueno,* bye."

As soon as Matty hung up, the phone rang. A recording asked, "Will you accept a collect call from…"

"Darryl Mínguez."

"Okay, yeah. Mingo? What's up?"

"Listen, babe, you know that little matter I asked you about before?" Like Mingo, Matty knew the phone lines into the pen are monitored electronically. He didn't need to tell her he was talking about the late Gordo Gonzáles.

"Yeah, okay, it's cool. Everything's cool."

Mingo sighed. Matty's antennae went up. It was one thing for Mingo to ask her to look into a *primo's* death, but it was something else for him to nag her. But she knew better than to talk about it on an open line.

"Listen," Mingo said, "you comin' to Outta Joint at the Joint?"

"Oh, right, the yard event. That's, what, this Saturday?"

"Yeah. I'd *really* like you to be there, babe."

Matty's antennae continued to wiggle. In the four years Mingo had been in La Pinta, he'd never asked her to come to a yard event. After all, there was nothing between them anymore. Nothing to bind them but broken dreams.

"Okay, I'll be there, Mingo."

"Great! That's swell. Okay, I'll see you Saturday then. *¿Suave?*"

Mingo hung up the phone. "Yeah, she's comin'," he said to his companions. Like him, they were in greens. "Okay? Okay, Jaime? Okay, Spidey? Now, get the fuck off of my back."

"You done good, bro." Jaime grinned. "We ain't gonna forget it." He thumped Mingo on the back and sauntered off with the other inmate. Spidey's forehead was tattooed in a pattern of inky black webs.

"Mingo."

Startled, Mingo spun around.

"Buckets! Jesus Christ!"

"Ya got a smoke, Mingo?"

Mingo sighed. "Buckets, I ain't got a smoke. You couldn't pay me back if I did, you asshole. Ask the Man for some roll-your-own, will you? Go on, git outta here."

"I'll let you look at my roach, you gimme a smoke."

"You'll *what?*"

"I'll let you see my roach, Mingo. I caught him in my house a little while ago."

"Why the fuck do I wanna do that? Why the fuckety-fuck do I wanna look at some goddam fuckin' bug?"

"I wuz thinkin' we could have us some roach races. Doobie says they used to have 'em roach races all of the time."

"You gotta have some bread if you're gonna bet on 'em, Buckets. That's why you race the motherfuckers, so's you can bet on 'em. Oh, shit, lemme see your roach."

"Jes' a minute. He was here a minute ago." Buckets began rummaging through his pockets, looking for the roach. "Jes' a minute."

"Aw, go away, will ya? Git!"

Alone, Mingo stared unseeing at the obscenities scrawled on the wall beside the telephone.

Bright and early, Matty turned her attention to a new problem: how to locate an aspiring comedian. She called Al Montana in Albuquerque. Like Rodney Stone, Albert Montaño was an old friend from Santa Fe High. He had changed his name to Al Montana when he moved to the Duke City, where he managed a talent agency.

"Al! Hey, it's Matty Madrid."

"Matty! *¡Qué milagro!* How you doing?"

"*¡Así así!* How's things with you, Al?"

"Would you believe it? I'm getting divorced. Debbie's divorcing me."

"Hey, too bad."

"Listen, I can live without Debbie. I can live without her just fine. She's gonna take me to the cleaners, and that's okay, too. It'd be worth a bundle just to dump the little bitch. Only, would you believe, she's suing me for custody of Boopsie?"

"Boopsie?"

"Yeah, the dog. I raised that little mutt since it was a pup, and now she's trying to alienate its affections, the little bitch!"

It took a minute for Matty to understand Al meant his wife and not the dog. "Well, okay, Al…"

Al groaned. "Don't never get married. It's hell on wheels."

"Yeah, well, it's funny you should say that. I was talking to somebody yesterday. She's been married three, no, four times, I guess."

"'Hope springs eternal.'"

"Yeah. Listen, Al…"

"What can I do for you, Matt?"

"I'm looking for a comedian."

"Sweetheart, *nobody's* looking for a comedian these days. They all want gangsta rap, in-yer-face-type death metal. 'Less it's a World War II reunion, something like that. Then it's the big band sound or maybe country. Country's hot, ya know. Hey, I could let you have Tex Dooley and the Cactus Crooners and at a discount, too, seeing as how you're a friend and all."

Matty laughed. "I don't want to book a band, Al. I'm looking for somebody for a client, and he, the somebody, he's a comedian, Herbie Koren. Used to play some of the clubs in Albuquerque. Maybe you heard of him."

"Herbie Karr! Why didn't you say so! Yeah, I know Herbie. Everybody does. Makes Henny Youngman look like Oscar Wilde."

"So, where can I find him?"

"Jeez, he ain't been around in a month of Sundays. Tell y' what. I'll ask around. Let you know what I find out."

"Thanks, bro. You're a doll."

Having launched the search for Herbie Karr or whatever he called himself these days, Matty made some notes to herself about her other case, the wrongful death of Gordo Gonzáles. Of course, it wasn't her case until Mrs. Gonzáles forked over $250 as a retainer, but she might as well get started. She needed to talk to Buckets. Okay, she figured Mingo would arrange a meeting with him during the yard event. She needed to talk to Mrs. Gonzáles again. She also needed to see the incident reports on Gordo's death. Dodi could ask for them when she filed for discovery, but Matty suspected whatever reached Dodi's office through proper channels would be "revised" to reflect the party line.

She'd have to get a hold of the reports unofficially.

Matty dialed the Corrections Department's Central Office and asked to speak to Carolyn Nhung. When Carolyn came on the line, Matty suggested lunch. They met at the Feed Store on the Turquoise Trail, where they pigged out on Christmas tree burritos, smothered in red and green chile.

Carolyn had been a nurse in her native Viet Nam. She and her husband, an officer in the ARVN, fled Southeast Asia in a leaky boat to seek a new life in America. In spite of her training and experience, Carolyn had been unable to find work as an RN. She'd gratefully accepted a clerical position in the Health Services Bureau at Central Office. She needed the money, but even more she needed the Blue Cross benefits to which a state employee and her family are entitled. Willie Nhung was slowly dying of a drug-resistant strain of TB he'd picked up in a re-education camp near Ho Chi Minh City.

"Matty! I am so very happy to see you. Anita talks about you all of the times at meetings of the Sodality."

"How are you, Carolyn? How's Willie doing?"

A look of pain flashed across Carolyn's face. "The doctors say it will not be so long. I cry for him already."

"I'm sorry, Carolyn. I know how it is." Matty reached for Carolyn's hand and gave it a squeeze. "How do you like working for Corrections?"

Carolyn made a face. "Oh, my good gracious. Those people, they do not hardly work at all."

"Yeah, well, welcome to the wonderful world of state employment. You know we got more state employees per capita than anybody? I guess that way if half of them pull their weight, we'll maybe break about even."

Carolyn shook her head sadly. "It is all one big coffee break, eight to five."

"What about the Secretary of Corrections? What about him?"

"Gilbert Gurulé? Oh, the Secretary is a very nice man…"

"But?"

"Everybody say Secretary Gurulé is a marionette. The *marionnettiste*…"

"The puppet master?"

"The puppet master who pulls the strings is Warden Jenks. Everybody know."

"Harley Jenks. Yeah." Jenks had come to New Mexico from Texas, the thirteenth warden in as many years. Lucky thirteen. Mingo, who was eager to gripe about CO's, case managers, food stewards, nurses, and associate wardens, didn't have much to say about Harley Jenks. She wondered why.

"Carolyn, a couple of weeks ago, an inmate died in an accident at the pen."

"Isaac Gonzáles. Yes, I remember. Dr. Delattre was required to certify his death. He is one of Health Services' physicians, Dr. Edgar Delattre."

"I'd like to see a copy of the medical report."

Carolyn's eyes widened, but she didn't say anything.

"Carolyn?"

Carolyn Nhung took a deep breath. "Matty, *chérie*, I know I am sounding so corny when I say this, but we did not come to this country, Willie and I, to make the fast buck. And we did not come here to be tools of the devil." She looked around her, but the other tables in the tiny dining room were empty. Their waitress was in the kitchen. "I will send you the report, the full report, so you see with your eyes what I speak about."

The next day, an envelope with no return address arrived at Matty's house. Like all letters mailed in Santa Fe, it had been postmarked in Albuquerque. It contained a copy of Isaac Gonzáles's death certificate, identifying the cause of death as blunt force trauma. No surprises there. But the envelope also contained a report from Francis McGuire, the physician's assistant who had been the first person to examine the body: "Severe trauma consistent with a blow from a blunt object. Pressure marks on upper arms. Probable restraint by application to the upper arms of an object at least three feet in length during induction of trauma."

In other words, somebody held Gordo down while somebody bashed in his skull. The death of Gordo Gonzáles was no accident.

(HAPTER TWO

"Medical."

"Hi," Matty said, smiling into the telephone. "Maybe you can help me. I'm trying to reach Francis McGuire."

"Mac?" There was a pause. "He don't work here any more."

"Damn!" Matty tried a new tack. "He owes me a hundred bucks, too."

"Oh, okay. I heard he was applying for a job at Golden Sunset Retirement Village. You might wanna try there."

Matty called Golden Sunset on behalf of the Corrections Department and gave the director's secretary a glowing recommendation for Mac McGuire. "Oh, and by the by," she added, "he left some personal property here. I tried to reach him at his old number, but..."

"Just a minute. I got it right here." The secretary was as helpful as a boy scout on a busy corner. She gave Matty McGuire's address and phone number.

McGuire lived in a run-down apartment building on Cerrillos Road, number 5B. When he opened the door, Matty smelled the pungent odor of stale beer and cigarettes.

"Mac McGuire?"

"Yeah. Who are you?"

"My name's Matty Madrid. Nice of you to invite me in." She

pushed her way past him and into the apartment. The *New Mexican* was lying on a coffee table, open to the want ads. Matty sat down. Reluctantly, McGuire sat down, too.

"Mr. McGuire, I'm a private investigator." She gave him her card and also one of Dodi's. "I'm looking into the death of Isaac Gonzáles."

"That son of a bitch! I wish I'd never heard of him."

"Tell me about him."

McGuire lit a cigarette. "I never saw him until after he was dead. They tell me he was a real fitness nut, the kind don't want to see a PA unless he's dying. God! I didn't mean that."

Matty shook her head. "So, you were the first to examine the body?"

"Yeah." He took a long drag on his cigarette. "The rec officer found him. They didn't have a doctor on duty, just me. So, when they brought him in…"

"They brought him in? You didn't examine him at the scene?"

"Hey! I'm a physician's assistant. I'm not a medical examiner. Anyway, it was pretty obvious what the cause of death was. The poor slob's skull"—he gestured at his forehead with both hands—"was stove in like, you know, a paper bag a kid blows up and pops it. You could see bits of bone embedded in the brain. Rita, warden's secretary, she fainted, for God's sake. She came down to get the report and fainted just like that." He snapped his fingers.

"Okay, cause of death a blow to the head."

"Blunt force injuries, yeah, but I had to get cute, impress them with my smarts, right? So, I did a full external while we were waiting for the physician on call, and that's how come I found these pressure marks on the torso and upper arms."

"Like somebody held him down…"

"They held a heavy object across the front of his body so he couldn't move. Yeah. He couldn't move. The son of a bitch had to lay there and watch it coming." He popped open a can of beer.

"Could it have been a barbell? You know what I mean, the thing with weights on the ends."

"Yeah. They told me he was pumping iron when it happened. That's what gave them the idea for this cock and bull story about an accident. He was bench pressing and the bar slipped. Yeah, sure."

"You don't believe it?"

"Hell, no! That ain't what happened."

"Because of the, uh, pressure marks?"

"Pressure marks, hell! Because of the angle of the wound. Even if he could have managed somehow to drop the damn thing on his head, it would have come down at a ninety-degree angle". He demonstrated. "This was, like, at a forty-five-degree angle to the top of the head."

"Suppose he's on the bench, and he can't get up because somebody's holding him down, and somebody comes up behind him and whacks him. Would that be consistent with the injury?"

"Sure, and that's exactly what happened. I'd bet my life on it."

"And that's what's in your report?"

"Yeah, and I wish to hell I'd minded my own business." He lapsed into silence as he drank his beer. His cigarette smouldered in the ashtray.

"What happened?"

"Well, Rita, she took the doc's report to the warden's office, but Jenks wants to see the file, the whole enchilada, my report, too. Two hours later, I'm a security risk, escorted off the premises by three CO's. Bye, bye, Mac."

"But you could fight it! I mean, the state personnel board…"

"I'm not a state employee. They privatized medical services, remember? Anyway, I know what's gonna happen to me if I raise a stink."

"What do you mean?"

"Jenks's gopher, Salas, he told me to keep my mouth shut. He said if I go to the cops, Corrections will 'discover' some irregularities in morphine distribution, irregularities they'll lay right at my door-step. They got three 'witnesses' lined up to say I was dealing, three pillars of the community, Gallegos, Ruiz—for God's sake, Winnebago Ruiz, and Delayo. Delayo, God! I dunno why I'm telling you all this. I shouldn't be telling anybody. I lost my job, but, at least, if I keep my mouth shut, I'm breathing fresh air. Jesus! I wish to God I'd never left Roswell. You guys in Santa Fe are nuts!"

"Wait a minute," Matty said, ignoring his diagnosis of mass psychosis. "I wanna be one hundred percent clear on this. Were you dealing drugs?"

"Hell, no! Lady, I was a corpsman in Nam. I know what drugs can do to your head. I wasn't dealing. My God!"

"But they'll say you were. They'll say you were dealing. They'll manufacture evidence. They'll bribe or maybe intimidate a couple of witnesses to finger you…"

"Listen, lady, get this into your head. They got the scum of the earth over there at the pen, and only some of them's in greens. You got eleven hundred inmates, but you got a helluva lot more 'n eleven hundred crooks. Don't get me wrong. There's some good people over there, decent people, honest-to-God good people, trying to make a living the best way they can." He banged his beer can on the table for emphasis. "But Harley Jenks is mean as a pitbull and twice as ugly. The biggest crook in the pen, lemme tell you, lady, is the warden himself."

After Matty left, Mac McGuire stared unseeing at the want ads. He picked up the phone and called his girlfriend, Gloria. Glo was a rec officer at the pen whose shift started at noon. With luck, he'd catch her at home.

"Glo? Hi, honey. It's me."

"Mac? I gotta go to work in a minute."

"Yeah, I know. Just…just had to talk to somebody."

"Why? What's wrong?"

"There was a detective here." He paused to light another cigarette. "Mandy, no, Matty Madrid. She's working for a legal beagle named, uh, Dorothy Koren. I got their cards. She's asking questions about Isaac Gonzáles."

"Uh, oh. What'd you tell her? You didn't tell her nothing, I hope."

"Yeah, hell, I told her what I know. I don't owe them SOB's the time of day."

"Mac! You're not supposed to talk to anybody! Salas says…"

"Yeah, well, Salas don't tell me what to do. Nobody tells me what to do. I got enough of that in the army. Those SOB's, they took away my job, Glo, and somebody's gonna pay for it!"

"Mac…"

"Aw, listen, honey, I'm sorry, dumping on you. Listen, what say we go out tonight? I'll pick you up after you get off work, have a couple of beers, maybe come over to my place." He paused. "Glo? You still there?"

"I…I can't. I can't go out with you. Salas knows we been going out together. He told me if I wanna work, I can't see you no more. I need this job. I need it bad."

"Son of a bitch!" Angrily, Mac stubbed out his cigarette. "You're not gonna let him tell you what to do, are you? Are you? Glo!"

"So long, Mac. It was… it was lotsa fun." She hung up.

Mac slammed the receiver down. He picked up the empty beer can and hurled it across the room. He ran his fingers through his copper-colored hair. In another minute, he'd start to cry. He'd seen guys crying in Nam like little kids, lost in the jungle and they couldn't find their way home. He didn't want to cry. If he started to cry, he'd never stop.

He got up and stormed out of the apartment. Flooring the accelerator, he tore out of the complex, forcing an oncoming Riviera to slam on its brakes. The Buick's driver flipped him off, but Mac didn't see him. He didn't see anything as he raced down the highway towards Corrections' Central Office.

Matty drove over to the park to watch the children at play. In their childish laughter, she could almost hear the voice of Esperanza. But she couldn't think about her daughter. She had to think about the case. She tried to make some sense out of it. Gordo Gonzáles was dead. Officially, his death was an accident, and Gordo's mother wanted to prove the accident was caused by the negligence of Corrections Department employees. Nobody'd be surprised if Corrections wanted to bury its mistakes along with Gordo.

But McGuire said it wasn't an accident, and Mingo said pretty much the same. "Don't you believe everything you read in the papers," he'd said. She'd forgotten to ask him what he meant. Still, it looked like murder, pure and simple. Corrections was trying to cover-up a homicide.

Why?

Fear of liability? Probably, but you can't have it both ways. Maybe the department was negligent, and Gordo died as a result, and they wanted to cover it up. Or maybe Gordo died as the result of a deliberate act of violence and the department wasn't negligent. In that case, why cover it up? On the other hand, maybe the department's negligence opened a window of opportunity for the killer. Mingo said there was no CO in the gym when it happened. She needed to talk to Dodi about liability. Are you liable for somebody else's crimes? Or maybe Mac was lying, trying to get back at Corrections for firing him. Maybe he was fired for cause. She didn't know. Maybe…

Maybe it was aliens from outer space.

She watched a kid trying to scale the fence that separated Engine No. 5030 from the public. No. 5030 was a steam locomotive on permanent display in the park. Signs warned the public to keep off. But people always want to do what they aren't supposed to. If they plastered signs all over No. 5030, "Touch!" or "Come On Over," nobody'd pay any attention to it. Signs don't matter. That's why we have prisons. Every con she'd ever known, and she'd known a lot of them, every one of them believed the rules didn't apply to him. You want a new car, you take it or a million bucks or a woman or a man's life.

A woman yanked the kid off the fence and whacked him. Hard. "What's the matter with you!" she yelled. "Can't you read?"

Lots of signs, but sometimes we can't read them, like the signs in Spanish on the restrooms in the library: *"Damas"* and *"Caballeros."* What's the poor tourist from Poughkeepsie gonna do if he's gotta go?

Matty left the park to run a couple of errands on St. Michael's Drive. Stopping by One Hour Martinizing to drop off her cleaning, she bumped into Jo Ann Valdez.

"Matty! Just the person I been looking for!"

"Hiya, Jo Ann. How's my favorite cop?" They'd been roomies at the Law Enforcement Academy. Matty was a sheriff's deputy until Leroy Maes fired her for insubordination, but Jo Ann had become one of the city's finest. Where will the dove come to roost, as they say? *¿Quien sabe?*

"Aw, I'm okay. Gotta go on a diet, but, hey, what else is new?"

"Listen, I keep telling you, you worry too much. You look just fine."

"That's easy for you to say. You're, what, size six?"

"Eight, but, hey…"

Jo Ann sighed. "I gotta go on a diet."

"Sure. Gotta scram. Good to see you, girl."

"Matty! Wait up. I wanted to ask you maybe you'd buy a couple of tickets to the circus. It's to benefit the Policemen's Benevolent Society."

Matty hesitated a moment. "Well…yeah, sure. Put me down for a couple. I'm all for benevolence."

"Ten dollars, Matt."

Matty forked over a ten spot. "Hey, Jo Ann…"

"Yeah?"

"You still got a, what, cousin working at Huntsville?"

"Nah, Tony ain't at the Texas State Pen no more. He got him a job with Corrections over in Austin."

Bingo! "Listen, could you ask him something for me? Ask him to find out what he can about Harley Jenks."

"Warden Jenks?"

"Yeah. He was at Huntsville before he came here, I'm pretty sure."

"Ten-four."

Matty was hungry. She'd intended to lunch at Taco Bell, but Jo Ann's tickets took her last ten bucks. "What the hell am I gonna do with circus tickets?" She laughed. "My life's a zoo anyway."

Matty went home. Anita gave her a plate of dry soup, "Spanish rice," it says on the menu at the Tex-Mex tourist traps. She promised to fry up some *sopapillas* for dessert. That was the good news. The bad news was about Matty's grandmother.

"She's not so good, Matty. She don't know me. She thinks I'm Irma."

"Irma? My God, her sister's been dead forty years!"

"I know, Matty. I don't say nothing. I don't see no reason. She's in the living room. I think maybe she's asleep."

But Gran was watching television, the noon news on Q 13. When she saw Matty, her features twisted in terror. "Who are you?" she cried. "What are you doing in my house?"

Matty was stunned. *"¡Abuelita!* It's me! Marta! Don't you know me? I'm your grandaughter!"

"I don't know you! Go away! Leave me alone! Irma? Irma!"

Patting the gnarled old hands, Anita gradually soothed the old lady. Gran whimpered a little as Heartsill Cribb began his forecast. Tomorrow would be partly sunny.

Matty fled into the backyard. Falling to her knees, she began to weed. It felt good to touch the earth. The soil was alive with promise. Cousin Cipi had planted the garden when Matty and her grandmother moved into the house on Agua Fría. Thirty-seven years Cipi worked for Cedar Hills Landscaping in Santa Fe. Like the fabled alchemists of old, he could transmute base metal, the cold *caliche* of northern New Mexico, into gold. Must be in the genes, she thought, like blue eyes or hemophilia, a gardening gene dominant in generations of farmers toiling in the fields of Dos Alamitos, the mountain village in which the family had lived for centuries.

To Matty, on the other hand, gardening was hand-to-hand combat, a battle fought to the last survivor, alone against a Golden Horde of dandelions. She weeded as she lived, with passion, seeking to impose an order on the chaos around her.

"You gonna pull up all of them petunias, you don't watch it."

"Cipi! I didn't hear you. Oh, *Tío!*" She looked down at the vegetable waste around her, and she began to cry. Cipi put his arms around her and held her until the sobbing ceased.

Finally she spoke. "Oh, Cipi. I don't know what I'm gonna do. Gran…"

"You do what you always do. You go on, *jita*, you go on. For three hundred years we been in this country, ever since 1692. We gone through wars and everythin', Comanche raids and land grabs, they beat us when we talked the Spanish in the schools, your grandfather dyin' in the Philippines, your mama when she walked out, and little Esperanza, too…but we still here. We gonna make it. Jes' like them flowers. Smile for me, *jita*. There! That's better. C'mon in the house. Anita's got some *sopapillas* for you. You gotta eat something. You such a skinnyinnis!"

The *sopapillas* were hot and fluffy. Matty poked a hole in hers to let the honey drip inside.

We are puffed up and empty. But if the crust is broken, we can be filled with sweetness.

The phone rang. Matty licked her fingers and grabbed it on the second ring. "Matty, it is Carolyn. They know somebody copy the Gonzáles file. They think it is Mac McGuire. He was at Central Office this morning. He is very angry. Mr. Reese have to throw him out."

"Reese?"

"He is in-house counsel."

"Yeah, I met him," Matty said, remembering another case of hers in which David Reese had loomed like Sandia Peak. She suspected Reese was in the hip pocket of the Denver mob, but she couldn't prove it. Maybe Jenks wasn't the puppet master after all.

"Matty, tell me what to do!"

"Where are you? Central Office?"

"I am calling from Allsup's. The telephones…"

"I know. Listen, it's okay. It's gonna be okay. You go on back to work, but don't say anything, okay?"

"Matty…"

"For Willie's sake. Okay?"

"Okay."

Matty felt the prick of conscience. She'd used Carolyn's friendship, asking her to copy the Gonzáles file. You do somebody a favor, and they owe you. You ask a favor, and you're in their debt. That's the way things work in northern New Mexico. Maybe it's the last vestige of the frontier, like a barn raising or a quilting bee, everybody pulling together for the common good.

Carolyn Nhung wasn't a native of the north. She came from another world, as surely as if she'd come from Mars. Well, she'd chosen to live in New Mexico. It was time she learned some of the colorful local customs.

But what if Carolyn lost her job? What if Willie lost his insurance? What kind of a colorful tradition is that?

Matty shook her head. There was nothing more to do about the Gonzáles case, not until she spoke to Mingo at the yard event. She telephoned Al Montana.

"Matty, baby! Just gonna call you!"

"You got some news for me, bro?"

"Yeah, baby. I tracked down Herbie Karr for you."

"*¡Bueno!* Gimme the info."

"He's doin' a gig Friday and Saturday nights at the Kachina Klub, 9 and 11."

"The *what* club?"

"Hey, don't look at me. I just book 'em. I don't name 'em."

"Okay. The Kachina Klub on…"

"Central. Where else? East Central."

Al gave Matty the address in Albuquerque, and she promised to check it out.

Quickly, before she could change her mind, she dialed the number of the Museum of Indian Arts and Culture and asked to speak to the curator of Mesoamerican art.

"Ezequiel Frésquez."

"Zeke? It's Matty Madrid."

"Matty! How're you doing?"

"Hey, I was wondering…" She felt like a kid asking a guy to the senior prom. Ten years ago, there was no prom for Matty Madrid. She'd dropped out of school to have a baby. Earning your GED while holding down a fulltime job and raising a kid doesn't get you any invites to the dance. "Listen, I've got this case gonna take me to Albuquerque. Gotta locate a guy works in one of the nightclubs there. I was wondering, would you like to come along?"

"Working on a case and you need me to provide some cover." He laughed. "Hey, why not? Tell you what. I've been wanting to see the show at the Albuquerque Museum. Why don't we spend the day, or what's left of it anyway? Let's go to the museum, get some dinner, grab a couple of beers at the club. Pick you up in, say, half an hour?"

Half an hour gave Matty just enough time to shower and throw on a dress, a flowery print on black, and black T-straps. Her only jewelry was a pair of gold earrings Mingo had given her when Esperanza was born. When Zeke arrived, she threw a scarlet *rebozo* around her shoulders. The nights were crisp and cold.

Gran was napping, but Matty introduced Zeke to Anita. Cousin

Cipi popped out of the kitchen to say hello. As they were leaving, Tina and her sister came over, they said, to borrow a cup of sugar.

As Zeke and Matty drove away, Tina turned to her sister. "Nice guy," she said.

"Nice guy." Angie nodded. "Would you believe? Matty goin' out with a guy!"

Tina giggled. "Who you expect her to go out with? A gorilla?"

"Naw, I mean, you know. I dunno, Matty's been out with hardly anybody since Mingo walked out on her, you know?"

"Mingo!" Tina made a face. "I'm never gonna understand what she could see in a jerk like him. And after what he did to the baby…"

"Yeah," Angie agreed, "only don't forget the cops investigated and Human Services, and they didn't find nothing, nothing at all."

At the Albuquerque Museum, Luis Jiménez's heroic sculptures almost took Matty's breath away. She shook her head when Zeke told her "Vacaro" had been criticized by some Anglos. "You know, a Mex with a gun? Must be a *pachuco*." He grinned. He's got a nice grin, Matty thought. She forced herself to focus on the exhibit instead of Zeke's grin.

They went to dinner at the Sanitary Tortilla Factory, an unpretentious barn of a building in downtown Albuquerque with good food, good service, and good company. The Queen of Spain, if she'd visited New Mexico, couldn't have asked for more.

After dinner, they roamed about Old Town, playing tourist. Matty sometimes wondered if downtown Santa Fe was becoming an upscale Old Town, catering to tourists and driving out the locals. A lot of people said so. But Albuquerque, like Santa Fe, is growing, changing, itself a living organism. The Spanish settlement had absorbed the Americans, the soldiers, the cowhands, the merchants, the emigrants in covered wagons and U-Hauls. But Old Town remains a place where people live and work and love and die. As it has done since 1706, the church of San Felipe de Neri on Old Town's plaza still ministers to the faithful who light candles for the souls of the living and the dead.

They left the plaza as evening settled on the Duke City like a bird returning to her nest. Matty and Zeke climbed into his Jeep Wrangler and drove east on Central to the Kachina Klub.

They ordered a couple of beers and settled back to watch the show. A singer in a red dress that clung to her like Saran Wrap lamented a broken heart. "Not even Krazy Glue can mend it," she warbled. The MC hopped onto the stage to introduce "the one, the only and, appearing at the Kachina Klub for the very first, but we sure don't hope it's the last time, Mr. Herbie Karr!"

Herbie fit his ex-wife's description to a "T," short, balding, and sporting a plaid jacket in chartreuse, yellow, and pink. Matty had an uneasy feeling the plaid jacket wasn't part of the act.

"Good evening, ladies and gentlemen! Boy, I'll tell you, I had a tough time gettin' here tonight. You know those orange barrels?" Everybody laughed. Albuquerque's streets are in a perpetual state of disrepair. Orange barrels marking construction hazards sprout like mushrooms after rain. "I'm tellin' you the truth. A couple of 'em chased me all the way down Central. I pulled into the parking lot just before they could cut me off! Whew!" Herbie wasn't funny, but the audience was mellow. At the conclusion of his act, a wave of applause swept him off the stage.

Matty found the door to the dressing room ajar. Smoking a cigarette, the songbird read *People Magazine* while Herbie touched up his make-up. He had a second show scheduled at 11.

Leering at his unexpected visitor, Herbie said, "Well, hello there! You want my autograph? You can have any part of me you'd like, doll. Just say when and where. I'd park my car in your garage anytime."

"Stuff it, Mr. Koren." Herbie blinked. "Your ex-wife sent me. I figure you know why."

The songbird put down her magazine. This promised to be as interesting as the latest dirt on Britain's royals. Herbie swallowed. "I don't have it."

"Well, you're gonna have to get it, okay? Ms. Koren figures you owe her…"

"I know what I owe her, but I don't have it! Just as soon as I make the big time…"

"Yeah, well, she doesn't have that long."

Herbie was angry. "You think I'd work in a gyp joint like this," he said, "if I had any bread? My God! Every penny I've got has gone to…"

Herbie shut off the flow of words like a plumber. But Matty could guess what he'd been about to say. She'd noticed the tell-tale signs of addiction, the runny nose, the jumpiness, the raspy voice. She didn't expect a junkie would be able to come up with the money to satisfy Dodi's claim, but, at least, she'd located him. If Dodi wanted to file a complaint against him, she knew where to serve the papers. In the meantime, she gave him Dodi's number in case he wanted to contact his ex-wife.

As soon as Matty left, Herbie Karr turned on the thrush. "What're you looking at?" he demanded sharply. Like most of the women in his life, she ignored him.

Making his way backstage, Herbie hesitated before approaching Marcus Penner. Penner was grooving to the sound of Doomsday Machine. As the band's manager, Penner had dreams of glory. The Kachina Klub was only the beginning: a recording contract, MTV, a national tour. One way or another, Doomsday Machine was the winning ticket in Penner's personal lottery. In the meantime, he'd continue to augment his forty percent with a finger in the unsavory pie of the southwest's growing drug trade. The band was a good cover for illegal activities.

But there was a fly in the sweet ointment of success. Gloria Apodaca'd called him about Herbie Karr's ex-wife, the lip, and her investigation into Gonzáles's death. The lip had gone so far as to hire a private eye. The big guy up in Denver wouldn't like that, but he'd have to be told. There were a couple of loose ends Reese would want to tie up before the PI unravelled the whole operation. Lucky thing Gloria always told her troubles to Marcus. They'd palled around when he was in the joint and after, and it sure paid off. She'd come whining to him whenever she was upset. That's when she wanted the stuff, and Marcus was her connection. She didn't know that everything she told him went lickety split to Central Office. Too bad Gloria's IQ was just a few points higher than her bra size.

"Marcus."

Penner shushed Herbie. He wanted to groove with the music.

"Marcus, we gotta talk."

Penner sighed and limped slowly to a backstage corner. "Christ!" he said. "What is it now?"

"I need some stuff, Marcus. I need it bad."

"So? You know the drill. Gimme some bread and I'll…"

"I don't have any money, Marcus. Please. My ex-wife's putting the screws on me, and I don't have any money, but I gotta have it, Marcus. I need it real bad."

Herbie was beginning to sweat.

Penner could hear opportunity knocking. "Tell you what I'm gonna do," Penner said. "Seeing as how you're such a good customer, I'm sure we can work something out. Meet me in the alley after the last show. First off, I got a little favor you can do me. You scratch my back, I'll scratch yours."

"Yeah, sure, Marcus, whatever you say. You're a real mensch, Marcus. I'll never forget this. What do you want me to do, Marcus?"

"It's no big deal. I'd like you to have a little talk with your ex-wife for me."

"Dodi?" Herbie wiped his damp forehead with his handkerchief. "Gee, Marcus, I'm trying to keep outta Dodi's way. I owe her some money, see, and…"

Penner laid his hand on Herbie's shoulder. "Maybe I can help you out, wipe the slate clean, huh? But I want you to talk to her. Tell her she'll get what's coming to her. But tell her she's making a big mistake taking on this case at the pen. Tell her to call off her investigator, too."

"What case?" Herbie was bewildered. "I don't understand."

"You don't gotta understand." Penner was suddenly in Herbie's face. "Just get her off the case, and you can have all the stuff you want, okay? On the house."

"Okay, Marcus. Sure, okay. Anything you say."

Herbie scooted down the hall to the pay phone and dialed Dodi's number. Listening to the recorded message, he could hardly wait for the beep before speaking. "Dodi, listen. It's me, Herbie. I'll have your money real soon, I promise, but first you gotta do something for me. You got a case out at the pen, Dodi. I want you to drop it like it was a real hot potato. No lie. The gimp says you gotta. Drop it, doll, and tell that PI you got to take a hike, too. Okay, Dodi? Talk to you later."

Backstage, Penner smiled to himself. It was so easy, like taking candy from a baby. Only this time, baby wants some candy for the old schnozzola so bad he'll do anything to get it, anything at all.

Zeke ordered another round, but Matty insisted on paying. "It's coming off my income tax," she said. "Business expenses." They listened in companionable silence to the band. They didn't have any choice. Doomsday Machine's amplification system more than made up for what the group lacked in talent.

Matty and Zeke were about to leave when they were joined by Al Montana. Al wore a guayabera shirt and several layers of gold chains. He jingled when he walked just like Santa Claus.

"Matty! Baby! Am I glad to see you! I need you, baby. Need you in a big, big way."

Matty's eyebrows rose, but she didn't say anything.

"Here's the scoop, babe. 'Member me tellin' you 'bout Debbie?"

"Yeah, she's left you…"

"She's suing me for divorce, but what the hey. Nah, it's Boopsie!"

"You told me Debbie wants custody…"

"Custody? Listen, she stole Boopsie. She stole the goddam dog!"

"Al…"

Lowering his voice, Al leaned forward. "I wanna hire you, baby. I want you find Boopsie for me. I'll pay you anything it costs me, but I gotta get the dog back."

Matty was quick on the uptake. "$250 retainer and fifty dollars a day plus expenses."

Al opened his wallet and pulled out five fifty dollar bills. It was Zeke's turn to raise an eyebrow.

"You know where to reach me, baby. Anytime. That's my girl." Al gave her a peck on the cheek and darted off.

"Did I miss something?" Zeke asked. "Did that guy just give you $250 to find a dog?"

Matty stared in the direction Montana had gone. "Yeah, well, what can I say? Business has been going to the dogs lately."

Saturday was the yard event, Outta Joint at the Joint. The brain child of a local DJ, Outta Joint at the Joint encourages inmates' friends and families to mingle with their loved ones in the yard, enjoying the music and the barbeque and, most of all, each other's company. The men can act like ordinary Joes for a change. But ordinary Joes aren't strip searched before returning to their "houses."

As usual, Matty was late. The CO on traffic detail looked as cheery as a patient in a dentist's chair.

"Hey, Gómez," Matty asked, "what's the matter?"

"Oh, you know, Matty, sure as hell be glad today is over."

"How come? 'Cause you're on your feet all day…"

"Ain't that. Jes' so many visitors comin' in. With some of 'em, you never know. Hey, you never gonna know."

The parking lot at the South Facility was full, so Matty parked on an access road. Having locked the Browning in the Toyota's glove compartment, she cleared the metal detector without any trouble. It's illegal to bring a weapon onto the grounds of a correctional institution. Even the governor's bodyguards are supposed to surrender side arms before escorting him into the facilities. Sometimes they do, and sometimes they don't. But Matty never left home without it, just like American Express.

Passing through the visiting room, she stepped into the yard. A K-9 officer was posted by the door. Matty figured his dog was trained to sniff out narcotics. Everybody knows drugs are a problem in the pen, and some people say it's easier to get high inside than on the street. But a port-a-potty had been set up nearby. One look at the dog, and the mule would make a bee-line for the john to flush the evidence.

She found herself in a courtyard bounded by the Library, Education, Chapel, Medical, Visits, Vocational, and Hobby Shop. Two raised beds of grass about three or four feet high passed for landscaping. Must be hell to mow, she thought. An inmate sat on one of them. His arms were around a smiling young woman. Two little boys, about six and seven, amused themselves running up and down the sloping concrete sides of the bed.

On the other bed of grass, a couple of inmates had taken off their shirts to soak up some rays. They stared at Matty like kids in a candy store, whispering to each other in the incomprehensible Spanish of the islands. *Los cubanos,* she figured, remnants of the Mariel boat lift.

The small courtyard in which she found herself opened onto two large recreation yards, one on either side of the library. A softball field dominated one of them. The other contained a volleyball court and a horseshoe pitch. Behind the pitch, a makeshift stage had been set up where a rock group writhed in adolescent abandon.

Food stewards put out gallon containers of baked beans and potato salad under the watchful eye of the associate warden. The burgers he grilled were almost indistinguishable from the charcoal which fueled the fire.

"Matty Madrid! *¡Qué milagro!*"

Matty turned to see a bespectacled CO smiling at her. She recognized Manuel Tórrez, Mingo's cousin. One big, happy family. Some people say it's the same mind set makes a man a cop or a crook, but Matty didn't buy it. If you're good, you're good, and if you're bad, you're horrid, like the little girl who had a little curl in the middle of her forehead.

"Manny! Hey, how you doing?" She took note of his bars and added, "You're a captain now! Hey, that's neat! I didn't know. Congratulations!"

Captain Tórrez shook his head. "It's no big deal," he said. "My oldest, you know Judy, she wants to go to NMSU." He shrugged. "Means a little more money comin' in."

"Hey, cream rises to the top."

Captain Tórrez quickly changed the subject. "Looking for Mingo?" he asked.

"Yeah. He's around here someplace, I guess." She scanned the crowd. "Sure a lotta people."

"It's okay. You know, these yard events, they're a royal pain, but it helps to keep down trouble. Nobody wants a write-up…"

"A write-up?"

"A disciplinary report before a yard event. You get a write-up, you get locked down and miss out on all the fun. You know, we had a warden a while back cancelled Outta Joint at the Joint. Remember? Damn near started a riot."

"You know what they say, 'Don't roil the water,'" she replied.

Moving through the mass of people, Matty stopped to say hello to some familiar faces. From across the yard, Big Nose Onís hollered at her, "Lookin' good, pretty lady!" She flipped him off. Onís laughed uproariously. To Big Nose, life is a joke, and you gotta laugh, even when the joke's on you.

She saw Mingo eyeing two men in civies talking to a uniformed officer. "Hiya, babe," Mingo said, giving her one of his quick smiles.

"See them two dudes in duds over there?"

"Yeah. The big guy, the one like a Mack truck on steroids. Who's that?"

"Him? That's Warden Jenks."

"And the little guy?" she asked.

"That's his number two, Deputy Warden Salas. He's a gopher and all-around boy. The guys call him the Enforcer."

Matty looked closely at the two men. Except for Jenks' size, there was nothing unusual about them. You'd pass them on the street without another glance. Yet in his hands Warden Jenks held the lives of eleven hundred men and half as many staff.

Jenks was talking to Salas. The deputy warden's eyes darted about the yard as if he were looking for someone. He glanced in Matty's direction, and she dropped her gaze. She didn't know why, but she didn't want to call attention to herself.

"C'mon," Mingo said. "I want you meet Buckets."

In the cavernous gym, several inmates visited with their families. An inmate stood alone in a corner, his shoulders hunched and his hands in his pockets. He was humming to himself.

"This here's Buckets," Mingo said.

Buckets looked down at his feet. "You sure are pretty," he said to his muddy shoes.

Matty bridled until she realized Buckets didn't mean to be out of line. "You know that ad, the one with the fried egg?" Mingo asked her with a grin.

"'This is your brain on drugs.' Yeah, what about it?"

"If they'd scramble them eggs, they coulda been talkin' 'bout Buckets."

Buckets grinned, as if he thought it was pretty funny.

"Listen," Matty said, "do you remember a guy named Gordo? Gordo Gonzáles?"

"'Gordo', that means 'Fatso' in American. You know that? 'Gordo' means 'Fatso'."

"Yeah. You remember him?"

"Gordo's dead. He died."

"He died here in the gym, didn't he?"

"Not here. Gordo didn't die here." Buckets waved his arms awkwardly. "He died over there." He pointed to a weight bench. Matty stared in astonishment. For some reason, carelessness, arrogance, or parsimony, Corrections had failed to destroy the evidence.

"That's right. Gordo died on the bench. He was lifting weights…" She paused, hoping Buckets would pick up the narrative thread. "Gordo was lifting weights, okay? And one of them fell down and hit him on the head."

"Yeah, it fell down and made his head go plop. Like a tomato. You know what I mean? Like a tomato. It fell down. Foster made it fall down, and then it fell. Plop. You just ask Ruiz. You ask Winnebago Ruiz. He'll tell you."

"Who? Who did what? What happened?"

Buckets began to hum, a little off-key.

Matty and Mingo looked at the weight bench, but there were no bloody fingerprints or dying declarations scratched into the enamel. Still, the bench should have been handed over to the state crime lab after the "accident."

"Mingo, who's Foster? Does that name mean anything to you?"

"Yeah, hell, I know Foster. Ever'body knows him. Heavy dude, real heavy. C'mon. Let's go outside. I'm gonna show you Sweet Papa Foster."

Outside, in the fresh air and sunshine, children chased each other about the yard. A couple of inmates were standing at the gym door, listening to the band. Mingo nodded to the older man as they walked by.

"Who's that?" Matty asked.

"Señor Mustaches. He's head of La EME."

"The Mexican mafia?" Mingo nodded. "The other guy, who's him? Kid with a spider web tattooed on his forehead?"

51

"That's Spidey, Señor Mustaches' 'boy.'"

"His 'boy'? Oh, okay."

Having finished its set, the rock group packed up its gear and left the stage. Matty could hear the announcer screaming into the mike, "And now, folks, direct from Albuquerque, the one and only Doomsday Machine!"

They strolled over to the horseshoe pitch where a trio of black inmates was playing a game of horseshoes. One of them scored a ringer as Mingo and Matty watched. The other players whooped and hollered, but the man's face was as blank as a sheet of fresh carbon paper. Matty could see the tip of a scar running from his chin under his shirt. She found it hard to believe a man could be cut so badly and live. "That's Foster," Mingo said quietly, "Sweet Papa Foster. He heads up one of the gangs, the Black Knights."

"Lotsa gangs in La Pinta?"

"Is the Pope Polish? Yeah, hell, there's gangs. Maybe no Polish gangs," he chuckled, "but there's black gangs and Chicano gangs, Mexican gangs, white gangs. The Aryan Brotherhood…"

"Yeah, I've heard of them."

"You gotta watch your step around them, 'specially you a nigger or a Mex. It pays a guy to join a gang. Then he don't get bothered so much by shitheads. Anyhow, Foster's a Black Knight. He's *loco,* real nut case."

"You think he's capable of murder?"

Mingo nodded. "Honey, Foster's capable of anything. The guy's nuts, I tell ya. He thinks he's immortal."

"What?"

"No shit! He was up in Cañon City, and he got cut from his chin to his balls, and now he thinks he's immortal. Mean sucker. He'll slice you up like a banana and eat you for breakfast on his cornflakes. Y' know, I heard there was bad blood 'tween him and Gordo, but I don't know shit about it. I'll ask around. Maybe I can find out somethin'."

"This your lady, bro?"

In the din, an inmate had quietly come up behind them. Mingo blanched when he saw him, but Matty said, "Can it, bro. I'm nobody's lady but my own."

The burly inmate laughed, but the sound was as hollow as a laughtrack on TV. "Introduce me, bro," he demanded. "What you standin' there for like a lump on a log?"

"Matty, this is Jaime Gonzáles."

"Gonzáles?"

"Yeah, Gordo's cousin."

Grinning broadly, Jaime Gonzáles said, "I heard you was meetin' Aunt Erlene. You keep up the good work, sweet cakes. That way, your boyfriend here, he won't get no busted head like ol' Gordo. ¿*Suave*?" Still grinning, Gonzáles walked away.

"Mingo! What the hell's going on?"

Mingo told her to pipe down. "Gordo's cousin told me to get you to look into this, okay? He don't want nobody gettin' away with whackin' somebody in the family. Next thing you know, they'll whack him, too. They're real homeboys over in Goose Neck, always lookin' out for each other. That's why you gotta investigate Gordo's murder. Jaime says he'll shank me if you don't."

"*Shank* you! You mean that bozo's gonna kill you unless I find the sonofabitch wasted his cousin?"

Mingo nodded.

"Oh, for...so, where's he gonna get a knife—shank?"

"Ever'body's got 'em. You make 'em yourself. You steal 'em or somebody brings 'em in. All you need's a piece of metal s-o-o-o long." He held his hands about six inches apart. "Get some tape. You can always ask 'em in the library. Sometimes they don't know no better. Wrap it around. You got a handle."

"But the shakedowns…"

"They shake down the joint, find some shanks. It don't matter. A couple of weeks later, we're back to square one. That ol' lady behind you, keepin' time to the music, she could be stompin' one into the ground. Maybe one of them little kids, playin' in the sand. *¿Quién sabe?* Half the time, the goddam metal detector don't even work."

"Jeez! Okay, so Jaime threatened you. Why don't you tell somebody? Get him in lockdown, so he can't hurt you!" She wanted to say, "I don't want to lose you, too," but Matty never spoke to Mingo about their daughter, not any more.

Mingo snorted. "Be me in lockdown. Permanently. I'd have to go PC. You don't tell the Man nothin', babe. You do, you get fingered a snitch, a *rata*. And then…" He drew the tip of his finger across his throat.

"*¡Hijo!* All that crap about getting a contingency fee for yourself…" Matty was angry. She was scared, but she was also angry, and anger was a lot easier to handle. "Was that just a buncha bullshit?"

Mingo bit his lip. "It ain't true. There never was no contingency fee. I just tol' you that 'cause…'cause I didn't wanna tell you about Jaime."

"Yeah, big *macho* man. You're too ashamed to tell me you're scared shitless of somebody. Oh, for chrissake, Mingo! That's why Gordo's mom laughed at me when I asked her for a retainer. *¡Sanamabiche!*"

"Shit. Yeah, okay. So, now you know. You gotta solve this case, babe, or I'm history. You gotta do it for me."

"But Buckets says…"

"Yeah, can you imagine Buckets on the witness stand? We dunno if he's tellin' the truth. Hell, he don't even know. Anyhow, we dunno why Foster killed 'im. If he did."

"And we don't know why Corrections wants it hushed up. What's Foster to Corrections? And don't tell me he's Secretary Gurulé's homeboy." She surrendered to the inevitable. "Okay, Mingo. I'll see what I can do, but you gotta look into it this end."

"Yeah, sure, babe. Whatever. Hey, they're linin' up for chow. C'mon over and get yourself some grub."

"Nah, I lost my appetite. You go ahead. I'm outta here."

On her way out, Matty stopped to speak to Captain Tórrez. She wanted to know if he could think of any reason Corrections would try to cover up an accident. She decided not to mention the possibility of murder.

"Matty, Corrections's been sued so awful many times. And, you know, sometimes it's over a little thing like a guy wants Post Toasties 'stead of Wheaties."

"'Breakfast of Champions...'"

"You won't see none of these punks on a cereal box." He smiled. "But some of them suits are pretty serious stuff, like that guy with the headache they wouldn't let into Medical on account of he's got no appointment, only it turns out he's got a blood clot on the brain and cashes in his chips while he's waiting for a doc. You take a suit like that. Now, if the department's to blame, then the state's gotta fork over really big bucks, and somebody's gonna be first in line at the Unemployment tomorrow.

"But even if it's unsuccessful, a suit's gonna get in the headlines, and they don't like that. They're like cockroaches, you know, running around like crazy when you turn on the light. All them other state agencies gotta operate in the public eye, but the department, all they gotta do is say 'reasons of security' and you're never gonna hear beans about it. If the guy on the street only knew..." His radio crackled. "Gotta go. Keep well."

Frowning, Matty turned to leave. Lost in thought, she didn't see Deputy Warden Salas. He was watching her like a goshawk watches a cottontail.

(HAPTER THREE

Sunday is the one day in the week inmates are allowed to sleep in, and, from the look of things, most of them were still in their beds. The library was nearly empty. In one corner, Spidey was reading *La Opinión* to Señor Mustaches. The boss of the Mexican mafia had clawed his way out of the fetid slums of Juarez, but you don't need reading, writing, and arithmetic to do so, just some brains, some *huevos*, and a black hole where your heart ought to be.

In another part of the library, a couple of Foster's homies were playing dominoes. Mingo had wandered over to watch the game when Lady Luck smiled on him.

"Aziz!"

One of the domino players looked up in surprise as the guard who'd called out his name hung up the phone. "You got a visitor," the guard told him. He yawned.

Aziz got up to leave. "Aw, shit, man," his opponent whined. "Who gonna play wit' me now?"

Mingo slid into Aziz's vacant chair. "Yo, Washington. Shuffle them dominoes, bro, and let's play us a game, Lamar."

Washington glared at him. His hatred of any blue-eyed devil warred with the essential *homo ludens*. If he didn't play with Mingo, he wouldn't be able to play at all, and then he'd have to cold haul it on outta here.

Washington was bored. He was used to life on the streets. You live hard, you die hard. In the free world, a man like Washington was walking heavy. But here… He'd applied for a lot of jobs, but there were at least half a dozen applicants for every vacancy. He couldn't even make fifteen cents an hour picking up cigarette butts in the yard. That punkinhead Buckets did it for nothing. Man's got a paper ass.

The caseworker told Washington he could get some Good Time if he enrolled in Education. Good Time could cut a sentence by half. But when he'd tried to sign up for a class in horticulture, all the slots were filled. He'd been screwed, blued, and tattooed by the criminal justice system of these here United States. There wasn't much to do but hang out with the brothers, killing time.

Chattering away, Mingo shuffled the dominoes. Gradually, he brought the conversation around to Gordo's untimely demise. "'Course, I didn't know him much," Mingo said. "Me and him, we was from, like, diff'rent places. *¿Suave?* Uh, you know? I dunno nobody knowed him good 'cept his *primo.* I dunno nobody else."

Washington laughed. "Dat do depend, mah man, on what you mean by 'know.'"

"How's that?"

"You mean 'know' like, say, somebody you done met or you mean 'know' like d' Bible say."

"Yeah." Mingo smiled. "I get ya. Ol' Gordo had him a 'boy,' huh? Shit, I didn't know that."

Washington grinned. "Ah's fackin' you, man. You know Baekke?"

"Two Bits Baekke? Yeah, sorta. I dunno him very well. Little guy, ain't he?"

Washington's grin was even broader. "It's dem little 'girls' is so much fun. Two Bits—shit! He'd let a whole pod cool 'im out, one right after t'other, and never even break out in a sweat. Little shit enjoy it, too."

"C'mon. You're kiddin'."

"No, man. Ah ain't puttin' you on. Shit! Why you think mah ace, Foster…"

Mingo pretended to study the pattern of dominoes on the library table. It wouldn't be smart to show much interest in Washington's story. Somehow he knew that a narrator is compelled to entertain, like Sheherazade before her sultan.

Sure enough, Washington's tongue got the better of him. The brothers didn't call him Gatemouth for nothing. "Two Bits is Foster's punk. Shit! Anytime Sweet Papa want some ass, Two Bits come a-runnin' like a old dog after a bone." He chuckled. "Real dog, man, dat's what the ace is. But don' let him know Ah tol' you. He go upside mah face so fas…"

Mingo smiled. "Foster and a little white guy. I'll be damned."

"Shit. Two Bits's one of dese here equal op'tunity employers. First off, he was d' bean eater's punk, an' now he got a brother coolin' 'im out like he was d' doughnut and Foster's de hole. Next thing you know, he'll be down in d' sweat lodge, humpin' dem Injins."

They both laughed.

At lunchtime, Mingo had more to chew on than macaroni and cheese. If Foster and Gordo were rivals in love, then one of them had a solid motive for killing the other. Come to think of it, he'd noticed Two Bits hanging out with the Black Knights lately, and now he knew why. Two Bits Baekke was one of those kids slips outta his mama's belly and into the lovin' arms of trouble. He'd peel anybody's banana if the dude'd be his daddy.

Mingo frowned. Most killers kill for love or money. That he could understand. He could see himself wasting somebody for a million bucks. He wasn't so sure he'd do it for a woman. But if he ever whacked anybody for love, it'd be for a woman's love and not for the love of a man.

Mingo shuddered. He'd made a name for himself in the joint, a regular standup guy. Nobody tried to mess with Mingo, but he'd seen plenty of trains pulling into La Pinta. Sometimes the dude wanted to ride and sometimes not. Gang bangs were a dime a dozen in the joint. If Two Bits wanted to play hide the weenie, it was no skin off Mingo's nose or any other part of his anatomy.

As far as Foster's sexual proclivities were concerned, Mingo's grandfather used to say, *"Cuando no hay carne de lomo de toda como."* If I can't have red meat, I'll eat anything.

So, thanks to Buckets, Matty had a suspect, and now Mingo could supply a motive. Foster killed Gordo because Gordo was his rival. But that didn't explain who helped Foster do it and why. Probably some of his homies *¡Bueno!* But why was the department covering it up? An inmate who kills another inmate could end up on death row. Mingo couldn't figure why Warden Jenks didn't put Foster in the hole. It'd be months before the case came to trial. Even if Foster got off scot-free, he'd be out of Jenk's thinning hair for a while.

The next day Matty tracked down the doctor who'd certified Gordo's "accidental" death. Dr. Delattre had retired from full-time practice at the VA hospital in Albuquerque, but he worked part-time at the pen to supplement his government pension. Angie's boyfriend, who worked the day shift at Burger King, told her an old guy in a lab coat and prison ID lunched there three days a week. Maybe that was Dr. Delattre. Matty figured it was worth a try.

Matty poked her nose into the restaurant. An elderly diner in a stained white coat ate a Whopper with lip-smacking relish. She glanced at Sal, who was busing tables. Sal nodded and went on about his business.

Matty sat down across from the doctor. She could read his ID, "Edgar Delattre, MD."

"Hello, my dear, you're late," he said.

Since the good doctor didn't know she was coming, Matty figured he had her confused with somebody else. "Doc," she said, "I want to talk to you about Gordo Gonzáles."

Dr. Delattre blinked. "I'm afraid I can't place the name. Is he at St. Vincent's?"

"Gordo was an inmate at the South Facility. You certified his death two weeks ago."

"An inmate?"

"At the pen. Gordo Gonzáles."

"I'm afraid I don't understand."

Matty was perplexed. Even if the doctor was part of a cover-up, why would he deny Gordo's death altogether?

"Isaac Gonzáles. That's his real name. He died in an accident in the gym. A five-pound weight fell on his head, and you signed the death certificate. 'Accidental death.'"

The doctor frowned. "Did I? I can't seem to remember." He shook his head. "I don't remember Mr. Gonzaga at all, but if you say so, my dear, I'm sure that's what happened." He beamed at her.

Matty understood. The old man couldn't remember Gordo's death. He probably couldn't remember much of anything.

"Tell me this," she said. "If a healthy inmate died accidentally, would there have to be an autopsy?"

"Oh, my gracious, no!" The doctor was delighted she'd asked a question he could answer. "Why would anybody want to do that? It would only upset the family. And now, my dear, if you'll excuse me, I really must be going." Dr. Delattre picked up the car keys on the table and toddled towards the door.

Matty hurried after him. "Whoa up, doc! You got my car keys."

"Yours? Oh, dear. Are you certain?"

"You got my car keys, doc." Matty gently plucked them out of the doctor's hand. "These are mine."

"Oh, dear. I wonder…Oh, here they are! They were in my pocket all the time." He chortled.

Matty left the good doctor in the parking lot searching in vain for his car. She picked up her drycleaning and headed home, zooming down Cerrillos Road at 50 MPH.

A police car behind her turned on its red light and siren.

"Oh, shit!"

She was only going fifteen miles over the limit like everybody else. The occasional law-abiding tourist who drives thirty-five to forty in a forty-mile zone inevitably causes a pile-up because everybody else is doing fifty-five to sixty.

Matty pulled into the parking lot at Baja Tacos. The cop car pulled in behind her. To Matty's surprise, Jo Ann Valdez got out, but she wasn't carrying her ticket book. "Hi, Matty," she said.

"Jo Ann! For chrissake! You about scared me to death."

"Aw, gee, I'm sorry. I just didn't know when you'd be home, and I wanted to tell you the news."

"What news?"

"My cousin Tony. Remember? The one who works in Austin?"

"Oh, yeah. You talk to him?"

"He's here in town. He's visiting his folks, my Uncle Rudy and his wife, only she's not my aunt, I guess, 'cept they just got married. Anyway, you wanna talk, I'm on my way over to The Kettle to meet him now."

Matty wanted to talk to Tony Abeyta very much. She followed the black-and-white to The Kettle and chowed down on a chicken-fried steak while Tony talked to her about Harley Jenks. "He was with TDC twenty-eight years. They say it's on account of him the feds put a stop to the con bosses back in '72." He shrugged. "Started off as a guard and worked his way up."

"Huntsville?"

"He used to be at Huntsville, yeah, but his last job in Texas was warden of the new supermax in Germantown."

Matty whistled. "I've heard of Germantown. Isn't that where they put the incorrigibles?"

"Yeah." Tony nodded. "That's where they got the fu... 'scuse me, foulups, guys who can't make it in population. Twenty-four-hour lockdown. No privileges. Nothing. *¡Nada!*"

"Kinda like Pelican Bay."

"California? Yeah. 'Cept we execute 'em quicker 'n California. New bill in the legislature's gonna limit appeals. Consolidate 'em. Execute 'em in, maybe, six years. Keeps down the overhead."

Matty suppressed a giggle. "Must keep the ACLU hopping to keep up with you guys."

He sopped up some gravy with a piece of bread. "Buncha inmate lovers! It's okay them goin' on about constitutional liberties and so forth, but when some jerk throws a jar of piss at you 'cause he thinks it's so damn funny, you gotta figger he flunked high school civics."

"Some people'd say it's like letting the Nazis hold a rally. *¿Qué no?* You gotta let them do it. You gotta extend constitutional rights to the jerks, the *pendejos*…"

"The fuckups," Jo Ann interjected.

"…as much as to the good guys, if it's gonna mean anything."

"Yeah, well." He leaned back in his chair. "The framers of the Constitution didn't have to deal with the scum of the earth like we do. I mean, look at the whole idea of martial law. There's times what's good for the country outweighs the welfare of one lousy scumbag or even four hundred of 'em, 'cause that's how many Texas got on Death Row."

Matty had to agree that something must be done about the rise in violent crime, and, as Gordo's death indicated, improved recreational facilities for inmates wasn't necessarily the answer. "So, how come Jenks left Germantown? And don't tell me Santa Fe was a step up the career ladder."

Tony snorted. "He left Texas one jump ahead of the Rangers. Lotsa rumors he was letting the inmates run the show in exchange for a piece of the action, you know? Couldn't prove it. Nobody'd testify against him, but the governor demanded his resignation."

"Caesar's wife," Jo Ann said unexpectedly.

"What? Yeah, well, we got our own ways of doing things in Texas."

"I've seen the bumper stickers," Matty said with a smile.

"'Don't Mess with Texas'? Hell, yes. If Jenks got caught beating up an inmate or, say, maybe one of them, a real pain in the ass, you know, died in suspicious circumstances, hell, they'd give him a medal. But aiding and abetting inmates in illegal activities…"

"What do you mean?"

"What do you think I mean? Narcotics. Supposedly, Jenks was supplying half of Germantown with enough heroin to keep them all happy as a hog in clover."

Jo Ann's radio crackled, advising all units in the vicinity to proceed to a ten-seventy-one on Cerrillos Road: "Code Three." She offered to pay for her lunch, but Tony waved her money away. The black-and-white burned rubber as it pulled out of the parking lot.

Her companions left a little later. As they walked out, Tony said something funny, and Matty turned to him with a grin. She almost collided with Zeke Frésquez, who was on his way in. Zeke gave them a little salute, but he didn't say anything. It seemed to Matty that he glowered at Tony Abeyta as they passed each other in the doorway.

Matty was dumbfounded. It was almost as if Zeke were jealous. But, how could he be jealous? They'd only been out a couple of times. Mostly, she'd turned him down whenever he asked her for a date. Zeke was good-looking, bright, a nice guy. But, like a kid in foster care, Matty didn't feel like putting her heart up for grabs. When Mingo walked out, it was as if somebody cut her into little pieces. She didn't want to be hurt like that ever again.

Then why did a chance encounter irritate her like a mosquito bite begging to be scratched?

Matty was waiting in the left turn lane for the light to change when she suddenly realized there was something all too familiar about the address to which all available units had been dispatched. As soon as the light turned green, she zipped into the through lane ahead of a long line of cars. Cutting across traffic, she pulled into the parking lot at Mac McGuire's apartment complex.

Looking a little frazzled, a uniform waved her aside. He probably figured she was a resident. She'd no sooner parked than the SOC team arrived, and she watched them trundle their equipment up the steps. A cop in plain clothes, probably a detective, waved at them from the doorway of 5B. The SOC boys followed him into Mac's apartment.

Matty had a sinking feeling in the pit of her stomach. Mac was so angry when she'd interviewed him, and Carolyn said he'd stormed into Central Office soon afterwards. Why? What did he hope to do there? Had he taken his own life in despair? Wait a minute, she told herself. Anger and despair are two distinctly different emotions. Angry people seldom kill themselves, unless they take the object of their wrath with them, the wife, the boss, the mother-in-law. If Mac had shot up Central Office before turning the gun on himself, it might have been understandable.

She spotted Jo Ann Valdez talking to a young woman in a sweat suit. The woman was in tears. Matty felt it would be okay to interrupt. After all, Jo Ann wasn't conducting an interview. That was a job for the detectives.

"Matty!"

"Hey, Jo Ann. What's happening here?"

Before Jo Ann could answer, the young woman turned to Matty. She was sobbing so hard, Matty could barely understand her. "He's dead. Mac's dead! I told him not to talk about it. I told him!"

"Not to talk about what? To who?"

Belatedly, Jo Ann introduced them. "Matty, this is Gloria Apodaca. Gloria is—was—the dead guy's girlfriend."

"No, I wasn't." New floodgates opened, releasing a torrent of weeping. "Not any more. I told him I couldn't see him no more. They wouldn't let me!"

"Who? Who wouldn't let you?" Matty suggested they sit in her truck where "we can talk more comfortable."

Gloria looked at the Toyota, Matty's Red Menace. She seemed to realize that her interrogator wasn't a police officer. "Who are you? What do you want?"

"My name's Matty Madrid."

"The detective? Oh, my God! You're the reason he's dead. You bitch! You goddam bitch!" Gloria struck out blindly at Matty. Jo Ann seized her in a hammer lock, hollering to the uniform on traffic detail. All at once, Gloria ceased struggling and collapsed at their feet in a fit of sobbing.

The detective stuck his head out of Mac's apartment to see what the commotion was about. Matty didn't want to compromise Jo Ann, so she left. There wasn't anything she could do anyway.

But Gloria Apodaca had given her something to think about. Dispatch used the ten code for a shooting, ten-seventy-one. That could mean almost anything. Remembering the way Mac had been when she'd seen him, Matty assumed he'd killed himself. Maybe that's what Gloria meant when she said, "You're the reason he's dead." Maybe Matty's visit had pushed him over the edge and into oblivion.

Or maybe somebody killed him to keep him quiet.

Matty wanted a cup of coffee. She stopped at Mickey D's and called home to check on her grandmother.

"Matty, dear! I'm so glad you called."

"Nita? What is it? Is Gran..."

"Oh, your grandma, she's doing real fine today. Ever'body's fine. We was just watching Phil Donahue. You know she likes Phil Donahue."

"Then, what?"

"You got a couple phone calls is all. Just a minute." Matty waited impatiently while Anita found the message. "Here it is. You call Mr. Al Montana in Albuquerque. Montana? What kinda name is Al Montana?"

"He's in show biz, sorta like Fargo North Decoder. Okay. I got the number. I'll call him. Thanks."

"Okay, Matty. You call him. He already called here twice already, only I didn't know what to say. Oh, and that nice man called."

"Who? Zeke?"

"Him, but he don't leave no message."

Matty called Montana collect from the pay phone. Al accepted the charges eagerly. "Matty, baby! Have I got news for you!"

"Al? What is it? What's going on?"

"I found Boopsie! I mean, I found out where Debbie is. You go on over there and you'll get Boopsie for me. I know you will, baby. ¿No?"

Matty sighed. She had more important things to do than play dog catcher. On the other hand, she'd already accepted Al's retainer. "Okay, Al. I'll come on down…"

"No, no. You don't hafta do that. She's up in Santa Fe, her and the boyfriend. Friend of mine saw them checking into the Nighty Nite Motel a half hour ago. Probably under his name, Martínez, Jake Martínez."

Matty ordered coffee to go. On her way out, she thought about Zeke. Why had he called? She shook her head. They were so far from being a number they added up to zero.

Matty drove down Cerrillos to the Nighty Nite Motel. "I'm looking for a Mr. and Mrs. Martínez," she told the sleepy-eyed clerk.

The clerk glanced at the registration cards. "We got three Martínezes here. Which one of 'em you want?"

Mr. and Mrs. Jake Martínez were staying in room 112. Matty noted the Lincoln Continental parked at the door. Maybe Debbie's disaffection was not so much an affair of the heart as it was of the pocketbook.

Expecting to trigger a volley of barking, Matty knocked loudly on the door to 112. But Boopsie didn't make a sound. Neither did anybody else.

Matty knocked again. "C'mon, Deb. I know you're in there. It's

Matty Madrid. C'mon, open up."

"Awright, awright! Don't have a cow." Matty was surprised. She wouldn't have figured Debbie Montana a Bart Simpson fan. Saturday morning kid-vid was more her style.

Debbie Montana opened the door. Her hair was touseled, and she wore a man's shirt in lieu of a robe. The man to whom the shirt probably belonged lay in the middle of a queen-sized bed. He smiled like a cat in a creamery.

"My God, it *is* Matty Madrid," Debbie said. "What the hell do you want?"

"Tell her to come in, honey," the man said. "There's always room for one more."

"Stick it in your ear." Debbie snarled. "You can do it if anybody can." Trundling a cart of cleaning supplies, the maid raised her eyebrows as she passed by, but she didn't stop. Her family in Oaxaca enjoyed her funny stories about the crazy Americans.

"Deb, I'm here about the dog."

"*What?*"

"Boopsie."

"I know the damn dog's name. Whaddaya want the dog for?"

"Al wants her. He says he got custody…"

Debbie burst out laughing. "Al wants Boopsie? Al? Listen, Al Montana don't give a good goddam about that dog. He only wants her 'cause of Mrs. Robbins."

"Who?"

"Old lady Robbins. She had an apartment in our building. She told Al, anything happens to her, she wants us take care of the dog. She told him she'd set up a trust fund, $10,000 a year. Al don't want the dog. He just wants the dough!"

"He told me he raised her from a pup."

"Yeah, and he told *me* we'd be on Easy Street. Listen, there ain't no dough. Me and Jake, we checked it out. We come up here to Santa Fe to talk to her lawyer, Rodney Stein or something, and you know what he told us? The old bag left all her money to the Animal Companions' Association. The Animal Companions' Association, for God's sake!"

"What about Boopsie?" Matty asked.

"There was nothing in the will about Boopsie. Not a thing. It was all a con to get some sucker like Al to take care of the damn dog."

"Okay, so you won't mind if I take her back to Al."

"Take her?" Debbie laughed. "Listen, when I found out about the dough, I dumped her at the animal shelter so fast..."

"Where?"

"Here in Santa Fe."

"When?"

"Thursday."

"C'mon, baby. C'mon!" Martínez crawled out of bed. He didn't bother to put on a robe. "It's party time." Slipping his hands under the tail of Debbie's shirt, he whispered, "C'mon!"

"I'm comin', damn it. Just don't *you* come before I'm ready, you sonofabitch!"

Debbie slammed the door, but Matty was already half-way to the truck. She'd have to touch base with Rodney Stone, the late Mrs. Robbins' lawyer. If Debbie was telling the truth, Al probably wouldn't want the dog anyway. But Matty was duty bound to take Boopsie home to papa.

She drove over to the animal shelter. The clerk on duty found Boopsie's name in the files. "But you're too late. She was scheduled to be put down this morning."

"Shit."

"Wait a sec. Danny called in sick. Danny does the euthanasias, so I guess she's still here. You want me to check?"

Matty did. The clerk returned with a furry armful of mop which she deposited in Matty's arms.

"That'll be $25, adoption fee," she said.

"$25?"

"She's been spayed, so it's only twenty-five bucks."

Matty made a mental note to add $25 in expenses to Al's bill on delivery. In the meantime, she'd have to take Boopsie home. The little dog quickly settled down, but the frantic barking of a spitz in the back of a pickup followed them down the street like tin cans tied to a newlywed's car.

Tina was at the house, helping her mom clean the venetian blinds. She fussed over the little dog like a kid with a new toy. "Hey, Matty! What you gonna call her?"

"I'm not gonna call her anything. She's not my dog. Just keep an eye on her while I check on Esperanza, okay?"

Matty's daughter sat in the easy chair by the window, watching the hummingbirds at the feeder under the *portal*. All too soon these jewels in summer's crown would fly south to Mexico, leaving behind them the empty shell of a child, Matty's "Hope."

Suddenly, a small, furry cyclone blew into the room. Esperanza's vacant eyes tracked Boopsie as the dog cavorted about her chair.

"Matty, I'm sorry. I wasn't watching and she…"

"It's okay. Tina, it's okay! Look!"

Ten years ago, when Esperanza was only two, an accident had seriously injured the child. She fell down the stairs while Matty was at work. Mingo, the baby's father, couldn't handle it. He walked out, leaving Matty alone and lonely. But Matty's family was there when she needed them. Somebody was always in the house, looking after Gran and Esperanza when Matty went out. "One hand washes the other, and together they wash your face."

In summer, Esperanza watched the hummers feeding on the *portal*. That was all she did, all she could ever do. It was as if the soul of the little girl were bewitched, like a princess in a fairy tale, but no fairy godmother waved her magic wand to undo the spell.

Yet it seemed to Matty that Esperanza watched Boopsie at play.

The little dog went over to the child and cocked her head. After a moment, she flopped down beside the easy chair.

Tina giggled. "You got a watchdog. Esperanza's got a dog."

"Yeah, well, I told you. She's not my dog."

Matty made a couple of telephone calls. First she called Rodney Stone. Then she called Al Montana. She'd call Zeke as soon as she had a minute.

"Al? I got your dog."

"Boopsie? Matty, honey, you're an angel!"

"Yeah. You owe me for one day's work and $25 expenses. I had to bail her out of the pound."

"The pound? Debbie wouldn't have put Boopsie in the pound!"

"She found out Mrs. Robbins gave all her money to the Animal Companions' Association."

"Baloney!"

"It's true. I talked to her attorney. You remember Rodney Stone? Mrs. Robbins meant to set aside some money for Boopsie's care, but she was so sure you and Debbie loved the dog as much as she did, she changed her mind. Listen, when do you want me to bring Boopsie down?"

"Down? To Albuquerque? Hell, I don't want the dog. If Mrs. Gotrocks ain't gonna pay to keep Boopsie in champagne and kibbles, I don't want it. You keep it. Take it back to the pound, dump it, whatever. I could care less!"

From where she stood, Matty could see into Esperanza's room. The little dog lay at her daughter's feet. Somehow, taking Boopsie back to the animal shelter, into the arms of Danny who "does the euthanasias," was no longer an option.

But that name, "Boopsie," would have to go.

"Yeah, listen, Al, okay. You're a prince. I'll send you my bill. You owe me $75, fifty dollars a day plus expenses."

"¡No problema! Oh, and about Herbie Karr…"

"Not my case anymore. I got hired to find him. That's all. It's up to his ex how she wants to handle it."

"No, baby, it's up to the cops."

"*What?*"

"Herbie Karr's dead. OD'd. Shot himself full of pure H, so I heard, China Cat, or maybe it was coke. I dunno. Listen, babe, the check is in the mail and thanks anyway."

"*Bueno*, bye." Matty stood lost in thought, wondering how accidental Herbie Karr's "accidental" death had been. Two accidents and a suicide. But what was the connection between Herbie Karr and the others? Mac and Gordo, okay, but the only connection to Herbie was Matty herself, Matty and Dodi Koren. She rang Dodi's number, but the line was busy. Damn! She hadn't billed Dodi yet, and she didn't even have a retainer.

Boopsie watched as Matty went into the kitchen to see if she could find some hamburger. Tomorrow, she'd go to Salazar's and stock up on Gravy Train. She made a mental note to do so.

But she forgot to call Zeke Frésquez.

"Oh, Matty, I think Boopsie's a cute name. I mean, for sure."

"Tina! I can't call a dog Boopsie, for chrissake. Think of something else."

"There's Mopsy."

"Or Cuddles," her sister said. Matty made a face. "Or Muddles or Muggles or…"

"Ruffles?"

"Ruggles," Matty said. "I'm gonna call her Ruggles."

"Ruggles? What kinda name is 'Ruggles' for a dog?"

"I'm gonna call her Ruggles," Matty said, ending the discussion. She didn't know why the little dog's name was Ruggles. She only knew that it was. When push came to shove, Matty followed her instincts more often than not.

She dialed Dodi's number again. "Dodi! Matty Madrid. Listen, girl. Herbie's dead."

Dodi's voice was suddenly hoarse. "Herbie? No. Jeez…"

"I'm sorry. I just talked to Al Montana. Herbie OD'd."

"An overdose? Herbie? Are you sure?"

"Shit, I'm not sure of anything. Why? Wasn't he on the stuff?"

"Oh, yeah, I just, I thought maybe the mob."

"The mob?" Matty sat up. "Herbie was involved with the mob?" Dodi cleared her throat. "Only a little."

"That's like 'a little bit pregnant.' You are or you're not."

"Herbie liked to say he had the boss of the Denver mob wrapped around his finger like a cigar band. I didn't believe him, but…"

"Hey, the cops are looking into it, and it's got nothing to do with me." It didn't seem like the time to mention fees and retainers.

"It's funny, but I got a message from Herbie Friday night. He said to drop the Gonzáles case. He said to drop you, too, Matty, but I didn't think much about it. Oh, God, I hardly ever thought about Herbie at all except when he owed me money." Dodi hung up the phone and sat in silence, staring at the drawing by Eli Levin on the wall. Levin recently changed his name. Everything changes. She got up quickly and went into the kitchen to wash her hair.

Matty drove to Goose Neck in a blue funk. Thanks to the threat on Mingo's life, she'd agreed to take the case, but she wasn't happy about it. She skirted Glorieta Mesa at 80 MPH. Starvation Peak loomed in the distance, and she shuddered involuntarily. She'd heard about the Spanish soldiers who starved to death on the mesa rather than surrender. She didn't know if the story was true, but the loneliness of the mountain mirrored her own. *Tejanos* used to say there was no law west of the Pecos. Maybe there wasn't such a lot of it in the other direction either, at least not in Goose Neck, New Mexico.

Sonny was standing on the porch, cradling the Winchester in his arms like a small child hugging a teddy bear. "Momma ain't here," he hollered. "She's over to the church." Matty was surprised. Somehow, she couldn't picture Mrs. Gonzáles on the altar guild.

"Okay I wait inside?" Matty asked as she went in.

Sonny stared at Matty, but he didn't say anything. She figured he wasn't one for small talk. She didn't feel much like talking either.

"You got brown eyes," Sonny said suddenly.

"Yeah, well, it runs in the family."

Sonny placed the rifle in a corner. Matty resisted the urge to ask him if it was loaded. As he'd done the first time they met, he sat closely beside her. Matty opened her mouth to snarl at him when he suddenly grabbed her chin with one hand and kissed her, hard. The other hand plunged into her shirt.

Matty's hands were free, so she clasped them together and rammed them into Sonny's crotch. Sonny yelped and let her go. Matty jumped up, pulling the Browning out of her purse. She leveled the gun in the general direction of Sonny's heart—what little there was of it.

"You hurt me," he said. He seemed surprised. "You hurt me!"

He lumbered to his feet and lurched towards her. The pink bandanna had slipped over one eye, so he looked a little like a buccaneer. Matty was about to shoot Captain Kidd at point-blank range when it crossed her mind that this was a helluva way to impress a client.

"Hardhead! You git on outta here!" Matty heard Mrs. Gonzáles' voice behind her, but she didn't turn around. She had eyes only for Sonny boy.

Sonny blinked, staring at his momma as if she'd suddenly awakened him out of a sound sleep. "She hurt me," he whimpered.

"I'm gonna hurt you, you don't shaddup. Go on. Git outta here!" Sonny went. A tall, skinny man in black followed Mrs. Gonzáles into the room. "This here's Ordell Koonz," she said by way of introduction. "Brother Koonz."

Matty made a conscious effort to keep her voice steady. She

didn't want the old lady to know how much Sonny had scared her. "Mrs. Gonzáles, you know why I'm here. If I'm gonna look into your son's death, I need some more to go on."

"Whaddaya mean? You got all you need to know. Ikie was workin' out, and that blamed machine of theirs kilt him dead."

"Yeah, well, it's not always that simple. Tell me about Gordo. Did he get along okay with the other cons?"

Mrs. Gonzáles grinned. "Ain't nobody gonna mess with Ikie. They knowed he wuz on the payroll. They wuz all scairt silly."

That wasn't exactly what Matty meant by getting along with other people, but she let it pass. "They were scared of him. You mean because he was a big man and strong…" To most of us, the world is made up of friends and other people. To guys like Gordo, it's divided into enemies and everybody else.

Mrs. Gonzáles' grin was even wider. "Shoot! They was *all* 'fraid of Ikie. Nobody messed with my boy nohow." She seemed to be boasting about it like a straight A report card or a good conduct medal.

"I don't understand. Why were they afraid of him? You mean his size and reputation or was there something else?" Mrs. Gonzáles only grinned, displaying yellow teeth like a shrivelled jack-o'-lantern's.

Gordo's mother wasn't much help. She didn't know who his friends were and, to hear her tell it, he didn't have an enemy in the world. Those who might have hated him were too scared to do anything about it.

As she drove home, Matty swore she wouldn't be alone with Sonny again. She wiped her mouth on the back of her hand. Willing herself to change the subject, she puzzled over Mrs. Gonzáles' proud boast, "Nobody messed with my boy." Somebody did. She wondered about the man in black, Ordell Koonz. Mrs. Gonzáles called him Brother Koonz. Probably a bill collector, she reckoned, but he sure looked like an undertaker.

Ordell Koonz turned towards Erlene Gonzáles. She offered him a beer, but he shook his head. "Hardhead! Git on in here!" Mother Gonzáles didn't bother to get up. She didn't need to. Sonny bounded up the porch steps two at a time, scattering the chickens. He picked up the Winchester, which, in his hasty exit, he had left standing in the corner.

"Hardhead, git me a beer."

"Sister Gonzáles," the man in black said, staring at the floor, "this is the detective you hired?"

"Yeah, sure, Preacher. Her name's Matty Madrid. She's gon' make us all rich." Erlene chuckled. She grabbed the can of Coors out of Sonny's hand and popped it open.

The preacher didn't laugh. "She's over young," he said frowning.

"Shoot, Preacher, it don't matter, jist so's she gits the job done."

"Just so she gets the job done," he echoed quietly.

Matty spent the rest of the day talking to people who, like Mrs. Gonzáles, weren't much help. After supper, one of Anita's *delicioso* green chile stews *con* potatoes, Matty sat alone in the twilight. She tucked her bare feet beneath her and stared unseeing at the statue of Our Lady of Solitude.

She heard a noise in the kitchen.

In the dim light, Matty could see Ruggles at the back door. The little dog was quivering with excitement. Somebody was outside, and he was about to come in without bothering to knock. Soundlessly, Matty took the Browning out of her purse and slipped into the kitchen.

Ruggles growled.

Matty waited in silence. Better to let the stranger make the first move.

The dog sniffed at the door sill. She began to whine.

"Matty Madrid?"

Matty spun around. Ruggles barked frantically at a solitary figure outlined in the archway between the kitchen and the hall. While Matty stood watch at the rear, the intruder had come in the front door like a welcome guest. Matty aimed the Browning at his midsection and shouted, "Hold it right there, bro! I got a gun and I know how to use it."

The intruder raised his hands. "Don' shoot, lady. Jesus! I ain' gonna hurt you. I jus' gotta talk to you. Put the gun down, lady, okay?"

"Ruggles! Quiet!" To Matty's surprise, the dog stopped barking, but she began to growl again. Good. Maybe that would intimidate the guy, that and a loaded semi-automatic. Matty gestured with the gun towards a kitchen chair. "Okay, you wanna talk? Let's talk. Sit down, but don't do anything dumb, okay?"

"Jesus, lady! Okay, okay."

Matty turned on the kitchen light. She didn't recognize the slight, dark figure sitting across from her. He was very young, twenty, twenty-one. His hair was short except for a slender braid at the nape of his neck. She could see his forearms below the rolled-up sleeves of his shirt. They were covered with tattoos. The mark of a *pachuco*, his *paca*, a small cross tattooed on his wrist, caught her eye. His blue jeans looked brand-new, and he wore prison-issue shoes.

"My God! You're an inmate! An escapee! You broke outta the joint!" She held the weapon steady with both hands.

"Don' shoot me, lady! Okay? I tell ya, I jus' wanna talk."

She figured he was more afraid than she was, and that was a helluva lot. She allowed herself to relax a little. "Who are you? What do you want?"

"I know you, Matty Madrid. I know you Mínguez' *ruca*."

She wasn't Mingo's girlfriend, but she didn't bother to correct the error. "So?"

The escapee took a deep breath. "I know you lookin' into Gordo's murder."

"*Murder!*"

"*¡Ése!* I know how Gordo got wasted." Nervously, he looked around him. He was afraid of a lot more than a loaded gun in the shaky hands of Matty Madrid.

"How come? How do you know Gordo got wasted?"

He bit his lip. "'Cause I'm one of the *vatos* did it, that's how come."

"Ruiz!"

"How'd you… Buckets! *¡Estúpido!*"

Matty could have kicked herself. She'd forgotten all about Winnebago Ruiz, and now she'd put Bucket's life in danger. Ruiz would finger him to his *primos*. He'd be branded a snitch, a target for any inmate looking to prove himself a regular standup guy. Bye-bye, Buckets!

"Never mind how I know. You're Winnebago Ruiz. How come 'Winnebago'? And don't tell me it's your Christian name. There's no St. Winnebago on the calendar."

A shadow of Ruiz' cocky self emerged. "*¡Chale*, homes! I don' guess you meet a lot of saints in a PI's line of work an' shit."

Matty didn't say anything.

Ruiz shrugged. "They gimme that handle in jail. I was always stealin' the RV's, runnin' 'em down to Mexico, you know? Make a little money, have me a good ol' time, start all over. What am I gonna tell y'? It's a living."

"What are you doing in blues? For God's sake, you're no minimum."

"Yeah, well, that's part of why I'm here. Lady, can you point that thing someplace else?"

"I got it pointed just where I want it." Matty's face was grim. "*¿Suave?* Answer the question."

"*Y qué chinga.*" Ruiz sighed. "They put me in blues, an' I got sent down to the farm. It was part of the deal."

"Who put you in blues? Classification? What deal? I don't get it."

"You shut up a minute, I'm gonna tell you! They put me in blues, see? I'm a minimum. I go on down to Los Lunas, to the farm, an' they take a bunch of us dudes to the Lobo game in Albuquerque, kinda like a reward for good behaviour. ¿No? Only I'm gonna take a hike 'cause of what Delaney said. Okay?"

"Slow down a minute." Matty shook her head. "They let you guys go to the football game?"

"Yeah, it's supposed to be rehabilitation." He giggled.

"Only you escaped."

"Yeah, well, rehabilitation don' always work. What am I gonna tell y'? I tol' the bulls I hadda take a leak, only I keep on going." Matty wondered if anybody had even noticed.

"So, you walked away because of something Delaney said?" He nodded. "Who's Delaney?"

"¡Ése! He don' matter. Jus' a dude. Only what he said, that matters. Shit, that matters a whole helluva lot. Shit."

"'Kay, what did Delaney say?"

"He said I was dead meat. He said the word in the yard was I was goin' home in a box on account of because I helped 'em waste Gonzáles."

"Okay, some con's gunning for you and…"

"A con? Lady, don' you listen? Ain't no cons after me. Not yet anyhow. Jesus! The warden, Warden Jenks. He put out a contract on me. Suppose' to be a new guy comin' in tonight, Delayo, an' he's gonna kill me on account of the warden tol' him to, Warden Jenks."

Matty motioned for Ruiz to be silent. She had to sort this out. Winnebago Ruiz helps Foster kill Gonzáles. Then he's transferred to the honor farm at Los Lunas, and somebody tells him the warden at Santa Fe has put out a contract on his life. It didn't make a lot of sense. In fact, it didn't make any sense at all.

"Let's go back a minute. They reclassify you so you're minimum?"

"Yeah, well…"

"Your points. You gotta have low points to be a minimum."

"Yeah, well, they fix that up for me, see? An' I'm in for murder two, only they gonna fix that up. Lady, you got a smoke?"

She shook her head. "You mean they faked the records so your points go down, and you're reclassified minimum."

"Yeah."

"At Central Office?"

"Hell, I dunno. Yeah. No, they musta done it at the South Facility. Nothin's centralized no more. Warden Jenks… *¡Ése!* He musta done it hisself or else he got the Enforcer to do it."

"Salas."

Ruiz was silent.

"Okay. Somebody cooks the books, sorta, and you're reclassified, so you get to go to the farm."

"Yeah, well, that was the deal. *¿No?*"

"What deal? That's the second time you've talked about a deal. Who made a deal with you? What'd you do to keep your end of the bargain?"

"Me an' Pico, we help the *cafuso* waste Gonzáles, an' we get a ticket to the farm. See?"

"The *cafuso?* The black? Sweet Papa Foster!"

Ruiz nodded.

"What does Foster get out of the deal? He goes to the farm, too?"

"He don' get caught. That's what Foster gets. He wants Gordo dead anyhow so's he could have his 'boy' all to hisself. Only he don' wanna waste 'im an' hafta sit in the hole six months waitin' trial. *¡Chite!* Can't entertain your 'girls' if you doin' T-time in T-Pod, can you?" He sneered.

"The hole, solitary." He was speaking a foreign language, one without roots or derivatives. "So, you and Pico helped Sweet Papa murder Gordo. Tell me how it happened."

Ruiz took a deep breath. "They wasn't nobody in the gym 'cept us an' Gordo. An' Buckets," he added as an afterthought. "The Man seen to that."

"Seen to what? That there was nobody in the gym?" He nodded. "Go on."

"Me an' Pico, we took one of them bars and held old Gordo down while Foster give 'im a *chingazo* to the head. He ditches his shirt, only it ain't his shirt. Belongs to some dude got sent over to the blues, see, so they ain't gonna trace it to 'im. The Man, he thought of everything." He shook his head in admiration. "That's about it."

"'Kay. I understand why you did it, you and Pico, and I guess maybe I understand Foster's motive, too, from what you're saying. But I don't understand why the administration helped you out. That's *loco*, bro!"

"Helped us? *¡Ése!* They set it up. They set the fat dude up. It was all their idea!"

"Why?"

He shrugged. "What am I gonna tell ya'." Matty believed him. He seemed like the kind of kid whose sole concern is what's in it for him. He wouldn't worry about somebody else's motive. Matty would have to find that out for herself. She lowered the gun.

"So, you escaped from the Lobo game, only you came all the way to Santa Fe to see me. How come, Ruiz?"

"I figgered I don' got much chance out there with Jenks lookin' for me. *¡Chale,* homes! Too many ex-cons, Arthur Guy and them, wanna do the Man a favor. Wouldn't trust the Dodger no further 'n I could throw the mother. I figgered I tell you what's happenin', maybe buy me some insurance. I gotta get away. I gotta go to Mexico. I know lotsa people in Mexico. I'm okay down there."

Matty thought about it. Too many facts, too many angles to consider. Distracted, she let her guard down, and Ruiz made a sudden grab for the gun. Ruggles flew at him, sinking her teeth into his ankle. At the same time, Matty whacked his wrist with the gun barrel. She'd taken her finger off the trigger, so wielding the Browning as a blunt instument was handier than using it as the manufacturer intended. She hoped that wouldn't void the warranty. The force of the blow knocked the gun out of her hands. Matty scrambled for it while Ruiz backed towards the front door, jiggling his leg to shake off the little dog.

"Ruggles!"

Ruiz ran down the street. Matty locked both doors and tried them. By the time she had turned around, Ruggles was padding down the hall. The little dog curled up beside Esperanza's bed and went to sleep.

But there was no sleep that night for Matty Madrid. "Holy Mother of God!" she said to the image of the Blessed Virgin. She had to put it all together. For one thing, that was the only way to keep her pulse from racing like Al Unser at the Indy 500.

Sweet Papa Foster killed Gordo. Ruiz said Foster had it in for Gordo because Gordo stole his 'boy.' Pico and Ruiz helped him do it. Jenks promised them a ticket to the farm in return. The farm was a prison, too, but it was the land of milk and honey to an inmate at La Pinta.

Why did Jenks want Gordo dead? Gordo was no pussycat, but wardens have a lot of ways to bring an inmate into line.

A confidential informant says you're planning a break-out, Gonzáles. We're gonna have to put you in the hole.

What informant? Who's been rattin' on me?

Ah, that's confidential.

She'd heard so many stories about La Pinta. A warden could make a con's life more wretched than society ever intended. She'd even heard whispers of a goon squad, a gang of sadistic officers who would beat a recalcitrant inmate into submission. There'd been goon squads at the pen before the riot. But Matty didn't believe the rumors.

Most of the CO's she knew, like Gómez or Toya or Captain Tórrez, were on the level. Like kindergarten teachers or dental technicians, they were ordinary Joes trying to make an honest buck in spite of aching feet and broken hearts.

All at once, she looked at the statue of Our Lady of Solitude, and a half-forgotten verse from catechism class came into her head: *Proclaim release to the prisoners and captives.*

The Holy Child of Atocha, He was the patron saint of prisoners. The story goes that in the old days He went about the Kingdom of Castile carrying bread and water to the captives of the Moors. North of Santa Fe, a statue of the saint in Chimayó wears out its little shoes on nightly errands of mercy in the valley. Every month, the village women cobble a new pair for the Holy Child. After all, anybody who visits the poor and needy in New Mexico is going to wear out a lot of shoe leather.

Winnebago Ruiz, who had been on the wrong side of the law since the age of eight, hadn't been inside a church since he was baptized as a baby. Now, running for his life, he didn't stop to pray to El Santo Niño, and that was just as well. In spite of His reputation as a miracle worker, the Holy Child would have been hard pressed to help Ruiz now.

Ruiz zig-zagged down Agua Fría in his haste to get away from Matty's house. His ankle hurt like hell, and he wondered whether the dog had rabies or maybe distemper. He should have killed it. He should have killed the *ruca*, too, which didn't make a lot of sense. He'd gone to Matty in the first place to tell her about Harley Jenks. Somebody had to know the truth in case anything happened to him, a sort of ante-posthumous revenge. But Ruiz wasn't given to introspection. He couldn't remember why it had seemed so important to come all the way to Santa Fe.

He should have stayed in Albuquerque. He had *primos* there. He had lots of *primos*. They would help him get to Mexico. He'd be safe in Mexico. He'd hide in the mountains where Jenks would never find him. *¡Ése!*

He should have stayed in Albuquerque, but when the old geezer in a pickup offered him a ride to Santa Fe, it seemed like Fate was greasing the skids. *¡Y qué chinga!* He should have whacked the old guy and taken his truck. All he had to do was get to Mexico. He had lots of *primos* in Mexico, but he didn't know anybody in Santa Fe.

Ruiz couldn't run any further. His ankle hurt. For a young man, he was out of shape. He should have spent more time in the gym, working out, instead of hanging in the yard, whistling at the secretaries in their flimsy summer dresses. Ruiz stopped to catch his breath. His chest was aching, and he felt a throbbing in his temples which seemed to increase with every step he took. He walked on a little, but his legs were jelly, and he was afraid they would give out at any moment.

In his panic, he hadn't noticed which way he went when he'd dashed out of Matty's house. He couldn't remember where Cerrillos Road was, but he knew Cerrillos leads to the Interstate, and I-25 would take him to Albuquerque. All he had to do was reach the Interstate. For some reason, the state has neglected to post a warning to Interstate travellers not to pick up hitchhikers near the prison, which is about a mile east of the highway. In his blues, anybody'd take him for a working stiff. Ruiz laughed aloud. All he had to do was get to I-25.

A pickup turned the corner several yards down the road. Its headlights illuminated Ruiz, and he panicked. He forgot about hitching. All he could think about was Jenks and his henchmen. They were after him. They were everywhere. They were in Matty's house. That's why she pulled a gun on him. *¡Ése!* She was one of them. Ruiz wasn't very bright, but he had a vivid imagination. He hid behind a garbage can until the pickup passed. The driver shifted into fourth and quickly accelerated.

Ruiz stumbled along the road, concealing himself whenever he heard a car. He didn't know it, but he was walking away from Albuquerque and toward Santa Fe. Agua Fría, which takes its name from the tiny unincorporated village on the outskirts of the capitol city, runs parallel to Cerrillos Road. If he kept up the pace, he'd reach St. Francis Drive before morning. St. Francis, too, would take him to the Interstate. All he had to do was to keep on going until he reached St. Francis Drive.

But Ruiz' tired legs would not cooperate. He had to rest, if only for a little while. He found an overturned packing crate, and he crawled inside. He would just close his eyes for a few minutes, just a few minutes ...

"¡Eso es!"

Ruiz woke at dawn. He heard voices outside the packing crate.

"¿Donde?"

"¡Eso es!"

They had found him. Warden Jenks, his tentacles of crime extending like some fabled monster of the deep, reached into a box on Agua Fría to seize the timid heart of Winnebago Ruiz.

He bounded out of the packing crate, startling a couple of drunks who'd been planning to doss down in it themselves. Ruiz didn't see them. Numbed by terror and drugged by sleep, he stumbled onto the road and into the path of an oncoming egg truck. Blinded by the rising sun, the driver never saw him as he swerved to avoid a white dog sitting in the middle of the road.

The truck hit Ruiz at 40 MPH, tossing him like a beanbag. The trucker figured he didn't need any more points on his license and, besides, anybody could see the guy was pretty well dead. He gunned his engine and sped away.

The drunks looked at each other. Wordlessly, they disappeared into an alley.

Beside the broken body of Winnebago Ruiz, the white dog howled at the setting moon.

CHAPTER FOUR

When Cipi stopped by the house the next morning, Matty decided not to tell him about her nocturnal visitor. She didn't want to worry the old man unnecessarily.

"Gonna stay with Esperanza, *jita*," he said. "Keep your grandma company. 'Nita, she got somethin' goin' on over at the church."

"*Bueno, Tío.*" She smiled at him. "It's always good to see you."

"Musta been some excitement las' night, huh?"

"Cipi! What do you mean?"

He slapped his forehead. "Eh, I forget. You don't listen to KSWV. How you gonna know?"

"Know? Know what?" Did the morning news announce that Matty Madrid had entertained a walkaway at gunpoint?

"Charles Anthony Ruiz, an escapee from the Los Lunas Correctional Center," Cipi intoned, "was…"

"They got him!"

"Who? No, nobody got nobody, 'cept Mr. Ruiz, he got hit by a hit-and-run-over driver las' night. Right here on Agua Fría, jus' a few blocks from your grandma's house."

"Hit-and-run?"

"What's the matter with you, *jita*? You don't hear so good? That's what I been tellin' you. A hit-and-run-over driver, he hit Mr. Ruiz and run him over."

"Is he dead?"

"Oh, sure. Dead as a doorknob. You know, some of them people, they don't drive too careful no more. I think it's 'cause they got 'em automatic transmissionaries, one hand on the wheel and another one wrap around a beer can. It's a dirty shame it hadda happen here. *¡Chitón!* I hear your grandma comin'. She don't want to hear 'bout somethin' like this."

"Cipriano!" Ema Madrid greeted her cousin-by-marriage warmly.

"Emy, you sure are lookin' beautiful today."

"*¡Eso no cuaja!* I always know when you tell a lie. The tips of your ears get red all over like a beet's. I get you some coffee. *¿No?*"

Matty left them singing paeans to the miracle of instant coffee. To Matty, "instant coffee" was an oxymoron. Anyway, she wanted something more substantial for breakfast than the usual, toast and black coffee.

Funny, a man dies. You hear about it, and you're hungry. You'd think you'd lose your appetite. Must be something to the ancient custom of funeral meats, a reminder to the living that they themselves are not among the dead. Because I live, I eat; therefore, I am not dead, because I eat. Not memento mori, *but* memento vivere.

Remember, o man, that thou art dust. A dust that breathes and weeps, makes love, and feeds an appetite for life itself.

Do the dead hunger like the living? In Mexico, on the Day of the Dead, people set out little candies in the shape of human skulls, food for the souls of their dead.

Maybe only God is never hungry, nourished by the adoration of six-winged seraphim. Lucky for Him, He doesn't depend on us. We're too busy worshiping the almighty dollar.

Matty climbed into the Red Menace and turned the key in the ignition. An idiot light glowed brightly, reminding her the gas tank was almost empty. Stopping at Gasamat for ten dollars' worth, she spotted Dwight Anaya walking along Cerrillos Road. Dwight walked everywhere. He enjoyed walking, which was just as well. He couldn't get a driver's license. He'd failed the written portion of the exam fourteen times. Although a graduate of Santa Fe High, class of '84, Dwight had never learned to read above a first-grade level.

Too many who can read and write are no wiser for it, Matty thought. Like the old saying goes, "To learn to be a fool, you don't need a teacher." To Dwight, on the other hand, the world was an orange, to be peeled and slowly savored until its juice runs down your chin, filling the air with the fragrance of Andalusia.

"Hey, Dwight! *¿Qué pasa?*"

"Hiya, Matty." He grinned like a kid on Christmas morning. "Where you going? Can I come, too?"

"Sure, bro." She smiled. "I'm just going over to Tortilla Flats. I'm so hungry this morning I could eat a bear."

Dwight frowned. "Tortilla Flats. They sure got some good omelettes there. But just sausages and ham, I think, Matty. They don't got any bear."

"Hop in, bro." Matty screwed on the gas tank cap. *"¡Vámonos!"*

Tortilla Flats, on the southwest corner of Calle de Cielo and Cerrillos, serves breakfast all day long. From Dwight's point of view, it's a good way to do business. He stoked the inner man on an omelette with green chili and six flour tortillas while Matty chowed down on *huevos rancheros* and plenty of coffee.

Dwight asked the waitress to bring him a side of salsa. Sometimes Matty thought Dwight was fueled by salsa like a Galles race car on high octane gasoline. Between bites, Dwight asked her, "What you working on, Matty? Can I help you? You know I like to help you."

"Sure, bro. Dunno what I'd do without you." Dwight beamed. "I'm working on a case out at the pen. One of the inmates died in kinda suspicious circumstances." Dwight nodded as if he had understood. "Anyway, I need to find out everything I can. His mom wants to sue."

"Who was it died already? Somebody we know?"

"No, no, bro. He was from San Miguel County. Isaac Gonzáles." Dwight shook his head. "In for... I gotta find out what he was in for." She signaled the waitress for a refill. Some mornings, you need a bottomless cup.

"You should talk to my neighbor. She works out there at the pen. Maybe she could help."

"S'okay. I know lotsa people in Corrections."

"Her name's Glo Apodaca."

"Glo...Gloria Apodaca? You don't mean... Jeez!" She dropped her fork. "I've been wanting to talk to her! If she's who I think she is..."

"She's a officer out there, Matty. Glo's a rec officer. She's in charge of the recreation at the South, I think, maybe."

"Let's go. Okay? I gotta talk to Glo Apodaca. C'mon, I'll give you a ride home."

He gazed with longing at the uneaten portion of his breakfast. "Maybe they gimme a doggie bag," he said wistfully.

"C'mon, Dwight!"

On the way over, Dwight told Matty that Glo usually left for work while he was eating lunch. His kitchen window overlooked the street, and, like a lot of people living alone, he ate standing at the sink to avoid the hassle of washing up. Besides, he could watch the neighbors come and go, which was every bit as entertaining as daytime TV.

Dwight lived in an apartment over his sister's garage. That way, Linda could keep an eye on him without having him underfoot. She'd promised their mother on her deathbed she'd look after Dwight. In fact, Mrs. Anaya died twelve years later. Stuffing a plastic Santa into the chimney, she fell off the roof. Winter and summer, Linda left the plastic Santa in place as a tribute to her mother's memory.

Some people said it was a miracle that the old lady had lived so long in spite of her doctors' prognoses. Others said it was no miracle; it was relief at having dumped the responsibility for Dwight onto

Linda's capable shoulders.

The Anayas lived on a cul de sac just off St. Francis Drive. Dwight explained to Matty that Glo was in the duplex next door. "The Moyas, they live in between, only I don't see them so much on account of Mrs. Moya, she's sick, and Mr. Moya takes real good care of her, but he don't get out hardly at all." Dwight nodded several times.

"So, tell me what you know about Gloria Apodaca."

Like a dippy bird on a glass of water, Dwight continued to nod. "She's a rec officer, like I tell you. She's been working at the pen a real long time. She's from Peñasco, I think. That's how come you don't know her." To Dwight it was unthinkable Matty wouldn't know another *villera*.

"She got a boyfriend?"

"She usta. There was this red-head fella come 'round, only I don't see him so much no more."

"Mac McGuire."

"I dunno his name, only I don't see him for a long time."

"Anybody else?"

Dwight screwed up his face. Concentration was not his strong suit. "There was this other fella, only I don't think he's her boyfriend."

"How come?" Matty asked as she turned onto Millsap.

"He never stays very long. Just in and out and then he's gone again."

"What does he look like? You get a good look at him?"

"He's just a guy, Matty, only…"

"Only?"

"He walks kinda funny, gimpy-like, you know?"

Matty laughed. "Hey! The PC police are gonna get you for sure." Dwight's eyes widened. "It's okay, bro. It's okay. I'm just kidding. Anyhow, I don't know who that is. It's sure got nothing to do with me."

She was wrong, but she didn't know it, not even when she pulled up in front of the Anayas' and Dwight pointed out a man with a bum leg leaving Gloria Apodaca's house.

Dwight got out of the truck. "*Bueno,* Matty. I'm gonna take you to Glo's so you can meet her. It's okay. I don't gotta be at my job for a long time yet."

"You still bouncing at Dappertuto's?"

Dwight grinned. He loved bouncing. "I'm the bouncer, you bet, Matty. They let me eat my supper there, too, only I don't get no beer to drink, just coffee when I'm working, but that's okay. Sometimes, I get to throw the people out, but just the ones acting *loco*, you know? It's a lot of fun."

Matty shook her head. People come to Santa Fe from all over. They spend *mucho dinero* in the best hotels, restaurants, and shops, trying to cage the bluebird of happiness that fledged in the simple soul of Dwight Anaya.

She followed Dwight up the sidewalk to the duplex. Gloria tried to slam the door in Matty's face.

"Hiya, Glo," Dwight said. Gloria glared at him. "You better c'mon let us in. This here's my friend Matty. She wants to talk to you."

It was hard to say no to Dwight, especially when he had one of his size fourteens in your door. Gloria invited her unwelcome guests to make themselves at home. She didn't have much choice.

"Helluva thing about Mac," Matty said.

"Mac was good people. I miss him."

"Tell me about him."

"I don't wanna talk to you! If they find out…"

"Listen," Matty said. "Something's screwy at La Pinta, and maybe I can help. Tell me about Mac."

Gloria shrugged. "He always wanted to help people, ever since he was a little kid. He told me he wanted to be a doctor, only they didn't have the money, and, anyway, his grades weren't so hot. He went into the army, and they trained him to be a… a corpsman. So, after he got out of the army, he was a PA, a physician's assistant, you know? And he was working in Roswell at a private hospital down there, only it closed up when it went bust. So, he come to Santa Fe and got him a job with Corrections."

"At the South Facility."

"Oh, he worked all over PNM. You just go where they tell you, like the recreation director. They made him administrative assistant, so now Carl's gotta wear a tie and work in an office. Mac was at the South Facility when it… when it happened." A solitary tear ran down her cheek. She didn't seem to notice. "He told 'em what he saw. He told 'em somebody murdered Gonzáles, so they fired 'im." More tears followed like rivulets of melting snow. "It woulda been okay, 'cept he couldn't keep his mouth shut, and they killed 'im."

"Gloria," Matty said, passing her a hanky, "how do you know they killed him? Maybe… maybe it was an accident." Or suicide.

Gloria shook her head. "Mac wouldn't kill himself. That's what you're thinking. I can tell it. He never woulda killed himself. And it couldn't of been an accident. He don't even own a gun. He hates guns."

"It just doesn't make a lot of sense. I know he went storming into Central Office on Monday, but they wouldn't waste him just because of that."

"No, that wasn't it. They killed him 'cause he talked to you, 'cause he talked to a private eye about Gordo's death."

"He told them that?" It took a lot to astonish Matty Madrid, but Matty was surprised.

Gloria wadded up the sodden handkerchief. "Stupid! Mac didn't tell 'em. It was me. I told 'em he talked to you."

"You!"

"See, there's this guy. He usta be in the pen, only after he got out, me and him, we had a little thing going for a while, and I… I told him."

"Slow down!" Matty gestured. "What guy? Who're you talking about?"

"Gee, that's funny." Gloria frowned. "You just missed him. His name's Marcus Penner. He manages a band, Doomsday Machine. He was here a minute ago."

"Doomsday Machine. Name rings a bell. Go on."

"Marcus is a pusher."

"Coke?"

"Nah, H mostly. And he's in tight with somebody in Corrections, somebody involved in smuggling drugs into the institution. I dunno who it is, but every time I tell him something, it goes back to Central Office like I faxed it to 'em. He dunno I know, but I do."

Matty frowned. "So, how come you tell him what's going on? Why do you talk to him at all? You said your little romance is over." Gloria continued kneading the handkerchief. From time to time, she'd carefully smooth it out, only to wad it up again. But she didn't say anything. "My God! I got it," Matty cried. "You're a junkie. Penner's your connection, and you feed him information in return for the stuff!"

"I'm not a junkie!" Gloria snapped. "Junkies are, like, bums and streetpeople. I just... it helps me to relax. That's all. I'm really stressed out, working at the pen. I just need it to relax."

"Yeah, sure. Like the guy who drinks three six packs a day says he's no alky." Gloria didn't seem to realize she'd needed a fix so badly she sacrificed her boyfriend's life to get it.

There was a knock at the door, and Dwight jumped up to see who it was. "Hiya, Rita," he said. "Matty, this here's Rita Martínez. She works at the pen, just like Glo."

"Rita's warden's secretary." Gloria said.

"Rita! Yeah, Mac mentioned you. He said you saw the body, Gordo Gonzáles' body. He said you went down to medical to get his report and you fainted when you saw the body. ¿No?"

"I don't want to talk about it."

"Rita..."

"I said I don't want to talk about it!"

"Okay, okay. Here's my card." Matty pressed it into her hand. "Call me if you got anything to tell me. ¿Suave?"

Rita ignored her. "Glo, honey, I gotta get back. I'm on my lunch hour. I just had to see how you're doing. Okay?"

Gloria nodded.

"Back? Back to the pen?" Rita didn't reply. "Hey, it's Wednesday, visiting day. Listen, Gloria. Thanks for your help. Gotta go. Dwight, you're a doll."

Dwight grinned from ear to ear.

Matty drove to the pen at seventy miles an hour. She wouldn't have driven so slowly, only fifteen miles over the limit, but she had to think. In her eagerness to talk to Gloria Apodaca, she hadn't finished breakfast, so she stopped at Allsup's for a chimichanga. She managed to wolf it down between Allsup's and the pen, a distance of about a mile.

There was no CO on traffic detail. The pen was so short-staffed some posts were left unmanned. You could drive into the institution in a Humm-Vee, and nobody'd notice.

"Hiya, babe," Mingo said, when they met in the visiting room. "Lookin' good."

"We gotta talk. Is it safe?"

"You mean, is Visits bugged? Naw, too much shit goin' down all over the place. They can't bug ever'body. Only security in Visits is Daughtry over there, an' he's a asshole." He nodded towards a CO staring vacantly out the window.

Daughtry stirred himself to let out Señor Mustaches' visitor, a middle-aged woman who fondly kissed *el señor* goodbye. She departed in the company of two well-dressed young men.

"La Señora Mustaches?" Matty inquired.

"Yeah, and them's two of her 'sons.'"

Matty's ear caught the intended irony. "What do you mean?"

"Everytime she comes, she's got, like, a different 'son' with her.

Word is, *el señor* gives 'em all their marchin' orders when they come to visit. That's so's he can stay on top of things while he's in La Pinta."

"But the lobby officer's gotta have their names upstairs. They can't get in unless they're on the *señor's* visiting list."

Mingo laughed. "He's got maybe twenty 'sons', all of 'em 'tween twenty-five and thirty, and they all look alike. Ever' one of 'em is 'Frank' or 'Joe'. Hey, what's up, babe? Didn't expect to see you today."

"Listen, I gotta know what's going on. Winnebago Ruiz came to my house last night."

"Ruiz!"

"Shut up, will you? He confessed to killing Gordo. Him, Foster, and somebody named Pico."

"Pico de Gallo. That's what we call him, Pauley Gallegos, 'cause he's like a fuckin' rooster, a *gallo grande*. Wow! Case closed. Good work, babe."

"'Wow,' nothing. Ruiz said Jenks put them up to it."

"Jenks!"

This time the CO glanced in their direction. Matty wondered if he had overheard. She lowered her voice. "He said Foster killed Gordo 'cause he wanted his boyfriend."

Mingo nodded. "Yeah. I was gonna tell you I found that out. Two Bits Baekke was Gordo's 'boy,' only now him and Foster get to play bouncy-bouncy on account of Gordo's, like, outta the picture. But I never heard nothin' 'bout Pico and Ruiz. I don't get it. What's in it for them? Now, if it was some of Foster's homies…"

"Gallegos and Ruiz were promised a ticket to the farm."

"Promised? You mean… Holy Mother of God!"

"Yeah, promised. Warden Jenks tells them they'll be reclassified minimum and sends them to the farm *pronto*."

Mingo shook his head. "I don't know nothin' about it, Matty. Swear to God."

"Ruiz didn't know why Jenks wanted Gordo dead. He didn't ask. But somebody told him they were dead meat, Ruiz and Gallegos,

I mean, because Jenks put out a contract on them. Funny thing, Ruiz *is* dead. He was hit by a car a few blocks from my house."

"Jesus!"

"McGuire, the PA who examined Gordo when they brought him in, is dead. They say it's suicide. Even Dodi Koren's ex, a clown named Herbie Karr, he's dead. He OD'd the night I spoke to him. Jeez, Mingo! Gallegos! What about Pauley Gallegos? You know anything about him?"

"Pico got sent to the farm, just like Ruiz. Only somebody shanked him in the dining hall. He's dead."

"In the dining hall? There must have been a lotta witnesses."

Mingo snorted. "Nobody saw nothin'. Not a damn thing. Ain't no fuckin' witnesses. We're talkin' inmates, babe."

"What about this, what, Baker…"

"Baekke."

"Yeah, him. You think he knows something?"

"The little 'girl'? I dunno, Matt, prob'ly not. Two Bits is just a human fuckin' machine. He got no brains or nothin'. Just a rubber arse. Anyway, he's been in the hole a month. Stupid *pendejo* slugged a CO. She was tellin' 'im he can't smoke in the library, and Two Bits says, 'It's a free country,' and she says, like, 'For everybody 'cept you, asshole.' So, he hauls off and slugs her in the gut."

"Sounds like a little sweetheart. One more thing…"

"Fight!"

Inmates and visitors jockeyed for a ringside seat at the window. Matty and Mingo worked their way through the onlookers to see what was happening. Like kids on a playground, a crowd of inmates surrounded a couple of guys in the yard, egging them on. Spidey stood impassively to one side. There was no foot patrol in the yard. Short-staffing again, Matty figured.

Frantically, the CO in Visits tried to raise someone on his radio. "10-32! 10-32 in the yard!"

There was no response.

"Damn!" he swore in frustration, beating his radio on the wall in a futile attempt to resurrect the lifeless batteries. "Damn! Damn!"

The two inmates began to circle each other warily. Matty recognized one of them, Sweet Papa Foster. "Who's the other guy?" she asked Mingo.

"Three Legs Thoms."

"*Three* Legs?"

"Don't ask. You don't wanna know."

"10-32! 10-32!" Daughtry had thrown away his useless radio and was trying to raise South Control on the communications system in the "cage," the secure control center in Visits.

"10-32!"

"What's your 10-20?" Control barked.

"Visits! 10-32, Visits!"

"10-4. Stand by."

The sky above the yard turned black as thunderheads gathered in the northeast. The two inmates, Foster and Thoms, ceased circling each other and stood still. Foster's face was as empty as a dead man's.

"Omigod!" Matty cried. "A knife! He's got a knife!" In the fading light, she saw the gleam of a shank in Three Legs' left hand. "Mingo! Foster's just standing there. Why doesn't he do something! Thoms is gonna kill him for sure."

"He can't kill Foster, honey. Nobody can kill him. The dude's immortal."

"Mingo!"

"I told you, ever since he got cut so bad, ain't nobody can kill him. Man says he was baptized in his own blood, and ain't no weapon gonna pierce it, sorta like a second skin. He's gonna live forever."

"Oh, for…"

"Lock and load." Speaking into his radio, Captain Tórrez stood at Matty's shoulder. Unlike Daughtery's radio, the captain's was in good working condition. "We have a 10-80, armed and dangerous. Repeat: Lock and load." It took Matty a moment to realize the captain was about to give the tower the command to fire at Three Legs Thoms.

Suddenly, Thoms struck at Foster. Foster jumped back only to trip over his own feet. Twisting as he fell, he landed on his hands and knees. Like a kid playing "horsey," Thoms jumped on Foster's back, seizing him by the hair. The crowd pressed forward, into the tower's line of fire.

"Damn," Tórrez swore softly.

As a farmer butchers a hog at La Matanza, Thoms slit Foster's throat with one swift stroke. A fountain of blood gushed onto the pavement, spattering the cheering crowd. Foster slowly collapsed, dislodging Thoms. The big man lay still.

Scrambling to his feet, Thoms did a little victory dance until, losing his footing on the bloodstained pavement, he fell to his knees. Holding his arms apart, he lifted his face to the darkening sky like a saint in ecstasy.

Tórrez called Final Quarters, sending the inmates to their housing units. He ordered Thoms taken in leg irons and a belly chain to the maximum security unit at the North Facility. CO's carried Sweet Papa on a stretcher to Medical, although it was clear to everybody Foster was beyond Dr. Delattre's help.

"Get these people out of here," the captain ordered Daughtry, after chewing him out for misdirecting the emergency response team to Visits. On his authority as watch commander, Tórrez declared the facility in total lockdown.

But the shank that had killed Foster vanished like snow in summer.

At 2:00 in the afternoon, Manuel Tórrez went off duty. He stopped at Allsup's to call Matty Madrid. She figured he needed to talk and he needed to talk to someone who wouldn't carry tales to Central Office. They got together at Rodeo Nites to discuss the incident over a couple of cold ones.

"Whole place is going to hell in a basket, girl."

"Tell me what happened today, bro. I got the feeling there was a lot more going on than just another fight between a couple of guys who don't know any better."

Manny nursed his beer in silence.

"Manny?"

"You're right, girl. You're always right."

"'Cept when I took up with your cousin. *¿Qué no?*"

Manny smiled. "Oh, Mingo. Well, you know Mingo. You pick up a stray dog at the pound, you don't know it's gonna bite you or maybe save your life someday."

Matty thought about Ruggles, Esperanza's Ruggles, it seemed. Ruggles would never bite the hand that feeds her, but Ruggles wasn't Mingo, not even in a parallel life. Matty didn't believe in parallel lives anyway. Living one life is a hard enough row to hoe. "How come Foster and Thoms got into a fight? They hate each other?"

"No, that's just it. Never was no bad blood between 'em. I don't mean they was friends, just never had nothing to do with each other. Foster's black, Thoms is anglo," he said with a shrug as if that explained the absence of any meaningful social intercourse.

"So, what did they fight about? You know?"

Manny frowned. "One of my snitches says it was Thoms started the altercation…"

"You sound just like a cop."

"Okay, them mixing it up. Sweet Papa didn't have no choice 'cept to go along."

"Does that sound like Thoms? A troublemaker?"

"Why you ask me every question twice?" he demanded. "No, Thoms ain't no trouble maker, but he's a stone killer. Doing life for the murder of a state cop in Illinois."

"Illinois?"

"Interstate transfer."

"Still, Thoms could get the death penalty for this one, *no?* Murder of an inmate by an inmate?"

"*¡Simón!*" Manny nodded vigorously. "It's a capital offense. 'Course, some of these Santa Fe juries, they don't see it that way. Might give the man a medal instead."

"Environmental control."

"How's that?"

"Cleaning up the environment. A guy wastes Sweet Papa Foster… oh, never mind. It's just a bad joke, and I guess I didn't mean it." Tórrez smiled.

"Let me ask you something about drugs."

Manny's smile faded.

"C'mon, everybody knows there's drugs in the pen."

"Yeah, okay, it's true. I can't deny it. It's been a problem 'bout as long as there's been a pen. Visitors bring it in, spite of all our precautions." He chuckled. "Would you believe some of these guys smuggle the stuff in in their flies? The wife kisses 'em hello—we don't body search the visitors, you know—and they go to the john, take it outta their mouths and stick it in their fly. I mean, how much stuff you gonna stick in your pants without getting a helluva lot of attention?" He grinned. "Sometimes, I don't say it happens very often, you got a dirty officer or somebody. Maybe the cons set him up by getting him to do them little favors till he's compromised, like a birthday card for the wife, and then they ask him one big one. Maybe he just likes the extra money. Keeps him from working triple shifts so often.

"Only, lately, it's like a dam busted. There's a lot more horse than a couple of visitors could smuggle in. I don't care how much they got in the smarts department. Somebody's smuggling stuff into the joint in a big way. It's pretty well organized, and we can't get a handle on it." He shook his head.

"What about the State Police?"

"The administration won't call 'em in. What they don't know won't hurt Harley Jenks, you know?"

"You think the Mexican mafia…"

"La EME? I don't think so. It ain't got none of their trademarks. 'Sides, they're moving into methamphetamine distribution anyhow, your general, all-around purpose drug. You can pop it, snort it, or toke the stuff. Eighty bucks a gram. But we're talking H here, and more and more's coming into the southwest ever' day."

"Some people would say, it's okay if the inmates get high. Keeps 'em outta trouble. And it's okay if they freak out or OD, 'cause they're pretty much a waste of everybody's time anyway."

Manny Tórrez banged his fist on the table. "Don't you never say that! They're human beings just like you and me. They don't deserve…"

A young man in a flowered shirt seemed to materialize out of nowhere to sit down beside them. "Hey, wow, am I glad to hear you say that, Manuel." Like graffiti on Duke City walls, disgust was written all over Manny's face. For a moment, Matty thought he was irritated at the mispronunciation of his Christian name. Instead of "Mahn-WELL," the interloper said, "MAN-u-el," as if the captain were a handy guide for home improvement. His accent was as distinctively "New Yawk" as Manny's was Martineztown.

"Mr. Walls. You still in town?"

"It's Walz, Ira Walz." He glanced at Matty, who nodded, but didn't say a word. "You bet, Manuel. I've got three busloads coming in Saturday morning, and everybody's juiced up to take on the establishment. We'll demonstrate in front of the capitol building, build up a tape library for the evening news, you know, then roll on down to the state prison *en masse*. Don't you love it?"

"Demonstrate? Demonstrate for what?" Matty asked. Manny growled. He sounded like Ruggles when Ruiz was at the back door.

"No, no, no. Not *for* what—it's what we're against! The Coalition to Stop Senseless Violence. That's who we are. We're opposed to the death penalty. Do you realize the United States is the only frigging country except for Russia…"

"Let me see if I've got this straight," Matty said. "You got buses of people coming in from, where? Albuquerque?"

"All over, New York and LA, sheesh, DC…"

"Wait a minute! All these out-of-staters coming to New Mexico to tell us what to do. Is that right?"

"Hey, it worked in Mississippi, didn't it? The civil rights movement? Hey, I saw the movie. Anyhoo, we could use some red and brown faces in the crowd. Spice up the film clips, you know? 'Hands Across America,' that kind of thing. Whaddaya say, *amigos*?"

Matty stood up slowly. "Listen, *amigo*, we been looking after ourselves since 1540. Sometimes, we don't do such a good job, but that's our problem. We'll keep trying till we get it right. Meantime, why don't you go back to the Big *Manzana* and clean your own house before you start whining about the dust bunnies under my bed. We got a saying here, fella, '*Gato llorón no caza ratón.*' You hear me? Now, scram!"

Manny Tórrez doubled up with laughter. Walz clearly didn't know what to think, but his years at CCNY as a perpetual undergraduate had taught him one thing: Discretion is the better part of valor. He jumped up and backed away, bleating like a stuck sheep all the while.

"What's that about anyway?" Matty asked when Walz had disappeared.

"'A mewing cat don't catch no mice.' *¡Qué querido!*" Manny wiped his eyes. "Oh, it's Lucius Bissel. You know 'bout Lucius?"

"Bissel? Isn't he on death row?"

"'Administrative Segregation/Capital Punishment,' us enlightened professional types call it. Yeah, he kidnapped a young woman in Pie Town 'bout a dozen years ago, raped her a buncha times, killed her, raped her dead body, and stole four dollars outta her purse. Spent the money on a coupla beers."

"Real piece of shit."

Manny nodded. "Bissel's exhausted all his appeals. He's scheduled for execution day after tomorrow."

"Oh, jeez, that's gonna bring everything and everybody out of the woodwork. No wonder Ira Walz is here."

"Like laying a sugar trail for a colony of ants." He adjusted his glasses, which had slipped down his nose. "Anyway, Bissel's an example of what I was telling you. He's got to pay the price. 'Don't do the crime if you can't do the time.' Hell, I've heard inmates say so, 'specially to the fish. They get up here from RDC, Reception and Diagnostic, you know, the new guys, the fish. They get up here from Grants, and they think they're really something. But 'Don't do the crime if you can't do the time' don't mean you gotta do it in some rat-infested dungeon on bread and water, *suave*? Listen to me, sounding like a inmate lover." He looked a little sheepish. "Sorry, Matty."

She waved his apologies away. "You don't have to say you're sorry to me, and you're sure as hell no inmate lover. I read you loud and clear. They gotta do the time, but we gotta insure they do it someplace safe. That's just, well, that's just the way it oughtta be in this country."

"Yeah, and that means safe from drugs, too. I ain't no Miss Priss. You know that. But a guy on drugs, he ain't just a danger to himself. He could hurt one of the other guys, one of my own people. Hell! Excuse me, Matty, but there's AIDS, too. Not to mention the costs if he OD's and the lawsuits after that." He shook his head.

"If there's a pipeline into the pen and it's not just an occasional visitor or a staff member on the take, you know what you're saying?"

"Yeah, somebody's aiding and abetting narcotics distribution at the pen."

"More than that, bro. Somebody's running a drug ring, some mastermind, I mean. And that's gotta be stopped before it spreads like a, like a colony of prairie dogs in a vacant lot."

"Sometimes it takes a bulldozer," Manny said, draining his glass. "Nothin' short of a bulldozer's gonna do it."

CO Sosa went from cell to cell, sliding a food tray through the slot in each door. It was only 4:00, but that didn't matter. Because the facility was in lockdown, security had to act as food stewards. Serving each man in every pod at the South Facility would take a long time. Sosa's sergeant figured his unit officers might as well get started.

"Shit! Hey, Sosa, how come we cain't go grub in d' dinin' hall?"

"You know how come, Washington. Facility's in lockdown 'count of them boys fighting."

"Sweet Papa and Three Legs? Shit!"

"Listen, Lamar, you eat your supper and you don't gimme no crap, okay? Mínguez, here's your chow."

"Sosa!" Washington hollered through the slot in the steel door. "Hey! Yo, man, axin' you a question, man! Mah ace, Foster, he daid?"

"Ain't supposed to talk about it. But I'm telling you, you wanna get up a collection, send the boy some pretty flowers, you better tell them put 'In Memoriam' on it in great big letters, maybe 'bout a foot high." Chuckling to himself, Sosa moved along the tier.

"Aw, man! Shit, man! Mah ace, mah ace boon coon. You was goin' live fo'ever. You such a *bad* nigger." Beneath the topless towers of Illium, Achilles' lament for his dead companion was no more profound than Gatemouth Washington's for Sweet Papa Foster.

"Yo, dude," Mingo said from the next cell. "Bummer."

"Dey set him up!" Washington cried. "Dey set Sweet Papa up, and now he daid! D' man is daid! Aw, dat's messed up. Dat's so messed up."

"*¡Qué gacho!* Talk to me, bro."

"He don' got no beef with Three Legs. Shit, he don' hardly know d' fuckin' wood. Thoms! It was Thoms. He dissed mah ace so's he don' got no choice. He *got* to fight!"

"Man's always got a choice, Lamar."

103

"You don' und'stand. He got no choice. Foster gonna fight. Shit! He thought he goin' live fo'ever. Aw, Ace, for why you go and die?"

"What happened? I was in Visits, and I didn't see nothin' till it was just about over."

"I tol' you! Three Legs dissed him, dissed mah main man. In d' yard, front of ever'body."

"You mean it just come out of the blue?"

"He dissed him, man! I'm tellin' you."

"Where'd Thoms get the shank?" Mingo asked. "You got a idea?"

"Aw, man, I dunno."

In the next cell, an inmate said, "Th' Enforcer, Mingo. Th' Enforcer give it t'im. Yup."

"Buckets? 'Zat you, Buckets?"

"The Enforcer give it t'im," Buckets said again. "I saw 'im do it. I saw 'im, honest to Pete." He began to sing. "Jesus loves you, dum de dum …"

"Dey set him up," Washington declared. "D' Man done set Sweet Papa up and d' Man done beat him down. Ah'm goin' get 'em. Get 'em, it's the las' t'ing Ah do. Ah'm gonna get dem double-clutchers."

Mingo didn't pay much attention to Washington's empty threats. Foster dead was one less ingredient to spice the witch's brew of life behind bars. At La Pinta, the pot is always on the boil. Mingo didn't give a damn about Foster. But he was worried about Matty. He tallied up the body count: Gordo, an accident, Herbie Karr, an overdose, McGuire, suicide, Winnebago Ruiz, another accident, Foster, homicide, Pico de Gallo, another homicide. Santa Fe was beginning to look like Sarajevo.

Mingo didn't want Matty's name added to the list of victims. Somebody was willing to go to any lengths to keep a lid on this thing. If Matty got in their way…

He wanted to call Matty. He needed to warn her, but inmates

can't use the telephone when the facility's in lockdown. He could ask his *primo* to do it, but that's against the rules. Tórrez was a stickler for the rules, and, anyhow, he was off duty by now. Mingo hoped the lockdown would be lifted in a few hours. After all, Foster was just another con, another con to die a violent death in the yard. Hell, it's all in a day's work.

"Yes, Jesus loves you. Yes, Jesus loves you. Yes, Jesus loves you. Yes, Jesus love you. Yes, Jesus loves you. Dum dum dum diddle dee."

Inmates couldn't call anybody, but staff was burning up the lines in spite of the universal assumption that the phones at the pen were bugged.

The one person at the penitentiary who didn't worry about eavesdroppers sat in his office, staring at the phone. "I don't understand it," Jenks said. "Damn it! I told them to get a hold of him. I need to talk to him."

Deputy Warden Salas rose on cue and opened the door to the outer office. "Rita, sweetie, you get a hold of Reese?" Salas turned to the warden. "She told his secretary to have him call you ASAP, but she ain't heard nothing."

"Well, tell her to try again!" Jenks told himself it was a mix-up in communications. That sort of thing happens all the time. But it bothered him like a pesky gnat, one of those no-seeums endemic to Santa Fe in June. He knew he'd overstepped the bounds when he ordered Gonzáles killed, but, hell, he was Harley Jenks. He wasn't no gopher like Salas.

He growled at his deputy. "Your people found that shank yet?"

Salas shifted uncomfortably in his chair. "Not yet, we ain't. I got 'em shakin' down everybody's houses. We'll find it and God knows what all. Chill out."

"Goddammit! Don't talk to me like I was some teeny bopper. I don't want your promises. I want that shank. It wasn't supposed to go missing. You told me you had it all arranged, you and Bowles."

"Sure, okay, I…"

"You know what the cons call you, Salas? They call you 'The Enforcer.'"

"Yeah, I know." Salas loosened his tie. "That's okay."

"That's okay? That's okay! Only if you enforce, Mr. Enforcer. You get it?"

Salas was saved by the phone.

"What is it?" Jenks barked into the receiver. "Well, put him on, for God's sake. Stupid bitch!

"David! What the hell took you so long?"

Salas strained to hear both sides of the conversation, but David Reese's reply was swallowed up in Jenks' bellow. He sounded to Salas like a bull elk in rut. For a fleeting moment, Salas wished he were in the mountains instead of sitting in the warden's office. It'd be a real pleasure to be hunting elk about now. He wondered what Jenks' head would look like mounted over the fireplace.

"Hell, yeah! I told you we was goin' take care of that little problem, and we did. We got nothing more to worry about. Foster's dead, Ruiz is dead. Delayo took care of Gallegos, just like I said he would. You told me Penner got Gonzales' family to drop their suit… What? She what? Goddam sonofabitch! Yeah, sure. Sure, I'll take care of it. You tell the don he's got nothin' to worry about. I'm tellin' you, I'll take care of it!" He slammed the receiver onto its cradle.

"Salas…"

"You want me to take care of it?" Jenks glared at the deputy warden. Salas sighed. "*Bueno,* boss. What you want?"

Jenks' face was grim. "That private eye…"

"Yeah, Mínguez' girlfriend or something. I saw her at the yard event."

"Well, she's still poking her nose where it don't belong. She talked to Gloria Apadoca this morning. Penner heard about it from Gloria first hand, and he told Reese. The word from Denver just come down: Waste her."

"What? A woman?"

The warden's smile was glacial. "Ain't you heard? They got equal rights now. You give the Dodger a holler. I want her pushin' up blue-bonnets just like the nig." The smile grew wider, but its warmth never reached Jenks' cold eyes. "A cunt, and a nigger, a kike, a mick, and a coupla spics. There's equal oportunity for you." He guffawed.

Salas didn't say anything until he was in the secretary's office. "*¡Culo!*" he swore under his breath. "Fucking *culo!* You can go to hell."

Rita peered intently at the terminal in front of her, pretending she hadn't heard every word through the half-closed door.

The storm moved in slowly like a visitor unsure of its welcome. It started to rain about the time Matty left Rodeo Nites. She waved goodbye to Manuel Tórrez and stood in the wet, wondering what to do next. So much for New Mexico's turquoise skies and golden sunshine, she thought. *Probably all that weapons testing at Los Alamos. Two-headed cattle and acid rain. Maybe I'll write my congressman. Get him to stop it raining when I forget my umbrella.*

A couple of sheriff's deputies she knew invited her to have a drink, but she said no. "Real ruckus out your way last night," one of the deputies said.

"Yeah, well, what can I say? It's so peaceful in the country."

She went home, for lack of anything better to do. The rain pounded on her windshield like a smash-and-grabber, reminding her to replace the windshield wiper blades. As she walked in the door, Anita spoke into the telephone. "Just a minute. She just come in. You wait a minute, okay?" She handed the receiver to Matty. *"Hablando del rey de Roma,"* she said. *Speaking of the king of Rome...*

"Matty? Hey, it's Zeke."

"*¡Oh, chiste, Zeke!*"

"Want to go on a picnic?"

"A pic…Zeke, it's raining toads and frogs outside!"

"Pick you up about five." He hung up before she could say no. She figured he was joking, but at five minutes to five, Zeke's Wrangler pulled into the driveway. To Anita's horror, Matty didn't wait for him to come to the front door. She dashed through the rain and hopped into the Jeep, but before she could close the car door, Ruggles jumped onto her lap.

"Ruggles! Oh, shit! Your paws are all muddy. Dumb dog!" Matty hugged her to show she didn't mean it. "Zeke, this is *loco*!"

"You only go around once, Matty."

"For chrissake, that's a beer commercial. This is real life."

Zeke didn't say anything as he drove through town and up Hyde Park Road. By the time they reached the picnic area, the rain had stopped and the world smelled freshly laundered. Zeke unloaded a hamper from the back of the Wrangler while Matty spread an oil cloth on the redwood table. Ruggles played tag with a pair of yellow butterflies.

"This is absolutely amazing," Matty said, peeking into the hamper at fried chicken, baked ham, potato salad, lemonade, and chocolate cake. "Where'd you get all this stuff?"

"You didn't know I was a gourmet cook?"

"Uh…"

"Neither did I. I picked this up at Kaune's. Nothing but the best."

She laughed. "I mean, I don't deserve this. I haven't returned your calls. I haven't—I'm not so good at this any more."

"Why try, Matty? Go with the flow. Enjoy yourself."

The sky cleared as the storm danced toward the Jémez. Sunlight gilded the aspens on the hillside. A junco caroled overhead. Matty turned her head to listen to its song.

Zeke kissed her.

She jumped as if she'd been bitten by a coontail rattler.

"I'm sorry," he said. "You weren't ready."

She laid her hand on his arm. "Don't be sorry," she said. "You kinda took me by surprise, that's all. No… it isn't. It isn't all. I'm trying, I'm still, I mean I'm trying to get a handle on a relationship that was over a long time ago."

"If it's over…"

"Let me finish. In a way, it'll never be over. We had a little girl, Zeke, a beautiful little girl."

"Matty!"

"Her name is Esperanza. When she was two years old, she fell down a flight of stairs." *And into a nightmare from which I can't awake.* "After it happened, Mingo walked out on me. He couldn't take it. Her brain is jelly. She can't sit up or feed herself or walk or talk or fly a kite or chase butterflies or play the piano or go out dancing or find a cure for cancer. She's twelve years old, but she's a baby, and she'll be a baby the rest of her life."

"Oh, Matty, I'm so sorry. How do you manage?"

"Gran and cousin Cipi—you met Cipi—and 'Nita and Phil and the girls and sometimes Phil's little sister. Somebody's always with her. I won't put her in a home. I won't!" Her eyes flashed.

"Nobody's asking you to."

"Anyhow, Mingo walked out on me just when I needed him most, and I can't, it's hard for me to trust anybody after that."

"It's okay. I understand." He took her hands in his.

"And I'm not interested in one-night stands. You know what they say, 'A night of joy, a morning of sorrow.'"

"'*Noche alegre, mañanita triste.*' No one-night stands. Maybe an occasional couple of afternoons." He laughed to show he was only joking.

"So, let's just be friends for now. I'm sorry. Maybe friendship—"

He kissed her hands. "Friends it is."

"Let's talk about something else." He talked about his work at the museum, and she told him about Gordo Gonzáles. "The thing I don't figure is if Jenks is such a crook, how come the governor doesn't dump him? Seems to me he'd be a liability."

"Hey, you're talking to a state employee, remember? Just like the warden. Nobody in the Roundhouse pays much attention to the museum, thank God, not unless we had an interactive exhibit of Mapplethorpe nudes, but I can understand the mind set."

"What do you mean?" she asked. Ruggles jumped up between them, and Matty scratched her behind the ears. The little dog closed her eyes and fell asleep.

"You know, a while back the governor fired the warden at the pen."

"Yeah, they said he was incompetent."

Zeke snorted. "He was a Republican, and the governor's a Democrat. And if you're a Republican, and a Democrat's in the Roundhouse, you're incompetent until you change your registration and vice versa. Welcome to the Land of Political Enchantment."

"But…"

"I know, I know. It's a classified position, and that's supposed to keep the penitentiary out of politics. Hell, this is New Mexico. Some places, like Santa Catalina County, you can't even get a job washing dishes unless you're on a first-name basis with the *patrón*."

"So…"

"So, what does that have to do with anything?"

She nodded.

"Corrections is a mess, thirteen wardens in a dozen years. The governor doesn't want Juan Q. Public to know about it, so he'll keep a lid on any problems they have out there. It's okay to have a *baboso* in the warden's office so long as nobody knows, but, if the governor fired him, the whole story of his incompetence would be trumpeted on the front page of the *New Mexican*. They'd blame the governor, and he'd probably deserve it. You sling enough mud, some of it's going to spatter the Roundhouse. 'Perception is all,' you know."

"No, I don't know, but I get the picture."

"That's what I mean."

"Jenks stays in office so long as he doesn't embarrass the governor…"

"My lord, Matty!" Zeke sat up with a start, waking Ruggles out of a sound sleep. "It just dawned on me. Your investigation could do exactly that, embarrass the Roundhouse. You're opening up a whole can of worms."

"To catch a pretty big fish with. Yeah, I know."

After she said goodnight to Gran, Matty looked in on Esperanza. The child slept curled into a ball. Her mother reached over the bed rail to corral a wanton lock of hair. Lying on the floor beside the bed, Ruggles thumped her tail in a canine hello.

The phone rang, and Matty ran to answer it before the noise woke everybody up.

"Matty, it is Carolyn."

"Carolyn? You sound awful. You okay?"

"It is Willy. Willy is gone."

"*Gone!* Gone where?"

"Willy die today, Matty. You tell Anita, please. I don't want to talk to so much peoples."

Matty crossed herself without thinking. "Sure, Carolyn. Jeez. I'm so sorry. What will you do now?"

"I have a sister in Orange County, Ca-li-for-ni-a." She pronounced each syllable with equal emphasis. "I go to stay with her."

"*Bueno.* That's a good idea. Give yourself some time, and when you come back…"

"No, *chérie.* You do not understand. I stay with my sister. I do not come back. I do not want all this peoples killing peoples. '*Il fait cultiver mon jardin.*' Do you know what I am meaning?"

Matty didn't know, but she wished Carolyn well and promised she'd be at Willy's funeral on Friday. "Anything I can do, girl, anything at all."

Discomfited, Matty wandered into the living room. She sat by the window and kicked off her shoes. Turning on the light, she opened her textbook, but her eyes would not focus on the page. Matty was taking a class in psychology at the community college. Sometimes, she thought her life was a textbook case.

A car drew up in front of the house, but Matty was too deep in thought to notice. The driver doused the lights.

At that moment, the phone rang again. Matty padded into the hall to answer it.

"Matty Madrid?"

"Who's this?"

"This is Rita Martínez, Warden Jenks' secretary. Remember me?"

Matty raised her eyebrows. "Yeah, sure, I remember you. What's up?"

"Listen, I thought you oughtta know. Warden Jenks called Central Office…"

"And?"

"He talked to David Reese. Reese is in-house counsel to Corrections."

"I know who he is."

"Oh, okay. Reese told him you were sticking to this case like rubber cement. That's what he said, 'rubber cement.'"

"How do you know what he said?"

Rita cleared her throat. "I musta forgot to disconnect when I put the call through. Anyway, Reese said Mrs. Gonzáles' attorney had been told to drop the case, but she wouldn't do it. He said she'd got one warning already, and, anyhow, he could handle her. But he was worried about you. He said he knows you, and you're a maverick, and you couldn't be pressured. He said you couldn't be threatened or bribed or anything."

"Hah! Well, thanks for calling."

"Wait a minute, will you? Reese told the warden to take care of 'our little problem,' and Jenks told Salas—he's deputy warden."

"I know."

"Well, listen, Miss Know-it-all, you don't know everything. I talked to Hilly on switchboard, and she said Salas called Arthur Guy. They call him the Dodger. Guy murdered his sister-in-law, only he got out on parole in July, so he'll do anything Salas tells him. He knows Corrections can revoke his parole in a second. So, Salas says Jenks wants to put out a contract on you, and Guy told him…"

The air was riddled by a shotgun blast. Matty hit the floor.

"Matty? Matty! MATTY!"

Matty heard tires squeal as the shooter's car roared into the night. She got to her feet and stumbled into Gran's room. Gran whimpered in her sleep, but she didn't waken. In the back bedroom, Esperanza slept the sweet sleep of childhood. Beside her bed, Ruggles stood guard. Matty almost laughed to think she'd worried the telephone might awaken them.

Matty had been sitting in the rocking chair when Rita called. The rocker looked like a woodpecker's happy hunting ground. The window had been shattered by the shotgun blast, and a sliver of glass pierced the heart of Our Lady of Solitude.

"Matty! Matty, are you there?"

"Rita! I gotta hang up. I'm gonna call the sheriff. You saved my life, Rita. I owe you one." She hung up, but before she could search the Rolodex of memory for the sheriff's number, the phone rang again.

"¡Hola!"

"Lay off the pen, you bitch. You gonna die."

CHAPTER FIVE

Sheriff Maes reached Matty's house in less than fifteen minutes. His deputy, Agustín Ramírez, was there in ten. The expression on Gus' face was as icy as La Bajada Hill in a snowstorm.

"Whooeee!" the sheriff said as he surveyed the damage. "You don't reckon it was none of your dissatisfied clientele, do you? Some old biddy, you ain't found her lost kitty cat?" To Leroy Maes, females in law enforcement came in handy whenever the coffee pot was empty. After all, if the Lord God put Eve in an apron, that's surely where she belonged.

Matty decided to come clean. "Listen to me, sheriff. Right after the shotgun blast, I got a threatening phone call." She told him about the mysterious caller. She told him about Rita's phone call, too, but somehow she managed to imply that Rita was also anonymous.

As she spoke, Gus Ramírez stood behind her like her very own Secret Service. Gus was a good man to have on your side, but, right now, Matty figured she didn't need any protection, not with two sheriff's vehicles in the driveway. The light bars of both Chevys were flashing a blinding cacophony of red and white. A curious crowd began to gather across the street, patiently waiting until somebody came out in a body bag.

The sheriff scowled. "Matty, dear, you sure can be a pain in the ass sometimes. Reg'lar little hemorrhoid. Hell, back when you was a sheriff's deputy, I'd of like to hauled off and thumped you myself. But that don't explain why the deputy warden out at the pen's gonna want you killed."

So, Matty told him the story, almost all of it. She left out any mention of Mingo or Buckets. She could always say she forgot. Maybe she could say she was in shock, post-traumatic stress whatever.

Maes shook his head. "Son of a gun. We investigated that hit-and-run. Ramírez investigated, didn't you, Ramírez?"

"Sure did. Like you say, hit-and-run. Just a accident. Sammy over at Happy Time Liquors put me onto a couple of winos seen it happen. Guy—Ruiz—ran right in front of an egg truck. Never had a chance."

"What about Mac McGuire? I know his death's outta your juris-diction…"

Sheriff Maes glowered. "Anything happens Santa Fe County is in my jurisdiction. City dicks investigated, only you better believe I make it my business to keep my ear to the ground and a finger in the pie."

"So?"

"McGuire killed hisself. Ain't no doubt about it. Just…"

"What?"

"Well, funny thing is, the PD got the gun, o' course, a 357 Magnum, and McGuire's prints was on the grip, 'cept they wasn't nowheres else, not on the trigger and not on the barrel."

"What about the bullets?"

"Clean as a kid in a washtub on a Saturday night. Here's somethin' else funny. They don't know who the piece belonged to. There wasn't no guns registered to nobody in New Mexico named Francis McGuire."

"His girlfriend said he hated guns. She said he'd never have one in the house."

"Yeah, well, my wife thinks I'm crazy 'bout her meatloaf." He sighed deeply. "But it musta been McGuire's. Who else?"

"It wasn't registered to nobody," Gus said. "I mean, the serial number was all filed down, real professional-like."

Matty raised her eyebrows. "You send it off to Quantico? What does the Bureau say?"

Gus looked at the sheriff. The sheriff studied the toe of his boot. "Well, now, Matty dear, there wasn't no need to go off botherin' the Feebies. They got enough to worry 'bout, what with racketeering and a-tomic spies."

"Do me a favor," Matty said. "Do us both a favor, okay? And ship that 357 to the crime lab. See if they can raise the registration number. I think it's important."

Gus put in his two cents' worth before the sheriff could say anything. "Ain't no trouble, boss. I can send it off tomorrow."

"Nothin' in the budget for no special courier," Maes grumbled.

"I'll send it UPS." Gus grinned. "Shoot, I'll even send it Fed Ex. Fed Ex to the feds. That's pretty funny."

The sheriff surrendered. Leroy Maes was a lot smarter than George Armstrong Custer, and he knew when he was outnumbered two to one. "Okay, Matty. I'll send it off to D. C. Ramírez'll send it off for me. That'll give 'im somethin' to do. I'll put out an APB on Arthur Guy. If he ain't the shooter, he's prob'ly done somethin' else we can get him on. Maybe spittin' on the sidewalk. An' I'll talk to 'em over at the pen about this death threat, but don't get your hopes up."

"To tell you the truth, I don't expect them to level with you. But I figure you can kinda buy me some insurance. They know I've spilled the beans…"

"The whole enchilada," Gus said.

"…maybe they'll lay low a little while." She suddenly thought about Winnebago Ruiz confessing his complicity to murder as a form of insurance against Jenks and his goons. But fate, as usual, had the last laugh.

While the sheriff oversaw the crime scene investigation, Gus took Matty to Dappertuto's for a beer and "further questioning." Cousin Cipi volunteered to stay with Gran and Esperanza. "I don't sleep nohow," he said. "My eyes is so open, betcha I look like a hooty owl. Gonna make a big pot of coffee for ever'body. Sheriff, you want some, okay?"

"Good idea, Mr. Vigil," the sheriff said. "'Nother couple hours, and I can have my first cup of the day. Might as well prime the pump." He looked at his watch, and he sighed.

As always, Matty found Gus' company relaxing. Talking to Gus was like slipping into mineral springs at Ojo Caliente. He was such an easy-going guy. It was hard to be uptight when Gus was around. The only time she'd ever seen him on edge was when the mask of Quetzalcoátl disappeared from the Museum of Indian Arts and Culture. "Never could understand it," he'd said in horror. "Pieces of God out where ever'body can see 'em like them old Catholics and their relics, you know. Never understand it in a million years." In less than twenty-four hours, Matty'd found the missing mask, ID'd a killer, and met up with Zeke Frésquez.

Matty and Gus had gone into the sheriff's department at about the same time. In less than two years, Matty was out on her ear, but Gus kept plugging away. He'd gotten a citation for bravery a couple of months ago, facing down a stone killer to save a woman's life. Matty'd been meaning to ask him out to celebrate, but somehow she never got around to it.

A Tewa from San Lorenzo pueblo, Gus had succeeded in finding himself a niche in the white man's world. Maybe he'd even be sheriff himself someday, the first Native American sheriff of Santa Fe County. He'd become a legendary hero like the holy twins, the children of the Sun. Somebody in the pueblo would carve a Gus Ramírez kachina. She'd seen a Mickey Mouse at the Kachina House on Delgado. Hey, why not a sheriff's deputy?

Sometimes, Matty thought Gus' feelings for her were more than buddy-buddy. But, as she'd told Zeke, she wasn't ready just yet for hearts and flowers. Gus was a good friend, and true friends are as rare as virgin turquoise.

Dappertuto's was crowded. You'd think it was Saturday night. It looked as if every table in the house was taken.

"Matty! Sweets!" Rodney Stone waved them over. He introduced Gus to Dodi Koren. Trust Rodney to remember a little thing like introducing a gentleman to a lady and not the other way around.

Gus ordered Tecates and another J & B for Rodney. Dodi slowly sipped an Evian. Matty figured Dodi's marriage to husband number two, the health nut, hadn't been a total waste. But maybe abstinence wasn't so much a matter of physical fitness as common sense. The cops were cracking down on DWI's. The one thing New Mexico leads the nation in: DWI's.

"Dodi was just outlining your case, Matt," Rodney said, offering her a basket of tortilla chips. Matty filled in the details.

"Lovey," Rodney drawled, "why don't you confine your Holmesian endeavors to the quest for straying canines? 'Ms. Keene, tracer of lost doggies.'"

"¡Oh, chiste!" She stuck out her tongue. "You and Leroy."

"You gonna tell 'em or me?" Gus said. Matty shrugged her shoulders. Gus told the others about the attempt tonight on Matty's life. When he'd finished, he tipped his chair back and leaned against the wall, enjoying the satisfaction of a storyteller whose listeners hang on his every word.

"My God, Matty!" Rodney was horrified.

Dodi Koren was speechless. Matty guessed that didn't happen very often. Probably one of those things you learn in law school, how to say the right thing on each and every occasion just like Miss Manners. She said as much, hoping to liven up the atmosphere.

It didn't work.

"Matty," Dodi said suddenly, "I didn't tell you. I got a message from Herbie the night he died. He said to 'drop the case out at the pen.'"

"That's what Rita was talking about!" Toying with a slice of lime, Matty leaned forward. She forgot her beer. "Rita overheard Jenks talking to Reese, and Jenks said 'the family's lawyer' had been warned. He meant Herbie'd warned you or maybe he was talking about Herbie's death. Maybe that was supposed to be a warning. Dodi, you've got to be careful."

"I'll be okay." Dodi said.

"'My strength is as the strength of ten because my heart is pure,'" Rodney volunteered.

Dodi giggled. "Oh, Rodney! Tennyson?"

Gus didn't want to talk about Tennyson. "Seems to me," he said, "you ladies—folks—oughtta let things ride for a little while. You stirred up a hornet's nest, and them little buggers gonna sting."

Matty and Dodi exchanged glances. "What I need to do," Dodi said, "is get off my keister and file."

"You mean even if it wasn't an accident…"

"Sure! Same difference. It's still negligent operation of a building if they removed security, allowing the killer access to the gym."

"Ixnay, Dodikins," Rodney said, shaking his head. "The Tenth Circuit dismissed a similar case last year. The question is whether the general public is endangered by the negligence of the state. If the killer, Alonzo Foster, was gunning for a single individual, Isaac Gonzáles, then the state's not responsible. Civil disorder, yes. Personal vendetta, no. Ipso Post Toasties and all that. You have no case, I'm afraid, Dodi."

"But what about the warden?" Matty asked. "If we can prove Jenks and Salas ordered the hit, doesn't that change things?"

Rodney cocked his head. "Definitely a new ipso to factor in postly," he said.

Dodi choked on her drink. "Sure! It's a constitutional issue, isn't it, Rod? Denial of Gonzáles' constitutional rights?"

"To life, liberty, and the pursuit of Two Bits Baekke," Matty said under her breath. She'd forgotten all about Baekke.

Rodney nodded. "A 1983."

"I'll talk to Mrs. Gonzáles," Dodi said decisively. "I've been waiting until Matty's investigation was completed so I'd know precisely how to word the complaint, but, maybe, with the full panoply of the law behind us…"

Matty frowned. "Problem is, you file, and the papers'll nose it out. They'll run the story, and I don't know if that'll be a brake on what's going on out there or some kinda spur."

"Mixed metaphor, sweets. Tsk, tsk, tsk."

"Can it." Having passed English Comp last semester by a single percentage point, Matty didn't intend to think about mixed metaphors ever again. "Rodney!" she said suddenly. "I gotta idea!"

"Whoops-a-diddle."

"No, listen. We got a case of low lifes at high levels of state government. ¿No?"

"Can't prove nothin'," Gus pointed out. "All you got's the word of a dead man, and him a convicted felon."

"You're right as rain. We can't prove a damn thing, but we can sure insinuate a lot."

"What do you mean, ducky?" Rodney wriggled uncomfortably.

"You're in tight with some of the bigwigs at the Roundhouse. ¿No?"

"I may trip the light fantastic along the corridors of power, but…"

"Why don't you talk to the governor? Let him know what these *pendejos* are up to. The Roundhouse isn't a court of law. It's more like a court of public opinion. You won't have to prove anything above and beyond a reasonable doubt."

Rodney shook his head. "The governor'll back his man, Matt, Gilbert Gurulé. They grew up together, picking onions in the Mesilla Valley, two peas in a pod." He frowned. "Onions in a basket."

"But nobody says Gurulé's involved."

"He's Secretary of Corrections. If he knows what's going on at the pen, he's a crook. Otherwise, he's a fool. In any case, he's going to deny the veracity of your sources, and the governor will back him up. The gov cut his eye teeth on the milk of party loyalty, to coin a phrase, and Gurulé's his man."

"Shit!"

"But you've given me an idea…" The waitress appeared at their table, and Gus ordered another beer. Matty decided to drink the one she already had. A little warm beer never hurt anybody. The English drink it all the time. "The attorney general is a friend of mine. He was teaching constitutional law when I was at Yale. We worked together on the formulation of SB 91." He shook his head sadly. Gay rights legislation had bombed in 1993. Hysterical visions of drag queens teaching kindergarten kiddies put the kibosh on it.

"Isn't the AG under the governor's thumb?" Dodi asked.

"Sweety, Anson Hughes is under nobody's thumb. Man's done it all. Public defender, law school faculty, white shoe firm on Wall Street, district attorney in Bernalillo County. Until the election campaign, he'd donate one Saturday a month to the People's Rights Clinic in the South Valley."

Dodi stared. "I didn't know that."

"You're not supposed to. He didn't want people thinking he volunteered to polish his image as a man of the people. The fellow really, truly has a phenomenal dedication to the law and all it stands for."

"Talk to him," Dodi and Matty said in unison. Matty laughed.

Dwight Anaya hove into view, trailing Glo Apodaca and Rita Martínez in his wake like a couple of pilot fish swimming alongside a whale. Rita gave Gloria a little push to hurry her along. "What's so funny, Matty?" Dwight asked with a grin. Dwight always wanted to be in on the fun. It was his night off, but he'd come to D's, looking for a good time.

"Wasn't much. Just Dodi and me said the same thing at the same time is all."

Dwight started. "Oh, Matty! That means you gonna die the same time almost. *¡Válgame Dios!*"

"Sit down," Gus said laughing. "Take a load off your feet." Introductions followed. Pleading a court date bright and early, Rodney took his leave, but Dodi chatted happily with Dwight about the vicissitudes of the World Wrestling Federation.

Matty took the opportunity to ask Rita some questions. Rita canceled her order for a Virgin Mary and asked for a Bloody Mary instead. Sometimes, even a Latina needs Dutch courage.

"Rita, you saw the body, Gordo's body, when he was in Medical. *¿Qué no?*"

Rita took a big gulp of her drink. She shivered as if it tasted of gall instead of tomato juice. "I saw him, but I dunno it's gonna help you any. He was just… dead. Maybe you should talk to Glo. She found the body. Tell 'em."

"Yeah, I found 'im," Gloria muttered.

"Where?"

"In the gym."

"Where in the gym?"

The others stilled like actors captured in a freeze frame.

"Where in the gym?" Matty asked again.

Glo shrugged. "He was over on the weight bench. And there was just blood and, oh, stuff where his face was." She looked as if she wanted to cry.

"The barbell. Where was the barbell?"

"What? The weight? Oh, I didn't see it. It wasn't no place, 'cause I know I didn't see it. I can still see…"

"What did you do?"

"Do? I pulled the pin on my radio. A buncha CO's come runnin', and they got me outta there. Sgt. Bowles, he gimme plenty of grief 'cause I wasn't supposed to be inside. I dunno nothin' else. I don't." She gestured as if she wanted to push Matty away.

"Sure you do. You know one more thing you gotta tell me. You're the rec officer." She nodded reluctantly. "How come the rec officer wasn't in the gym?"

Gloria stared at Matty in terror. "He told me not to," she whispered.

"Who? Bowles? Who told you not to?"

"He told me to go to the ball field. He said maybe they need me to umpire."

"*Who?*"

"Salas. Deputy Warden Salas." Glo put her hand to her mouth. "I'm gonna be sick." She ran to the ladies room.

Rita started after her, but Matty grabbed her arm. "Rita, *dígame,* you got any idea what Gordo was in for? What was his crime?"

"I can't tell you that. Inmates' records are confidential. We don't even tell staff. That's how come some nurse got beat up by Fay Weller last year. Nobody told her he had this thing about blondes looking like his mother."

"His mother!"

"Yeah, he beat her up, too. That's how come he was in the pen."

Dodi Koren interrupted. "Matty, I think I can answer your question. I've seen Gordo's coat…"

"Jacket."

"Whatever. He was doing three to five for trafficking in controlled substances."

"San Miguel County?"

"All over northeastern New Mexico."

Matty was beginning to see a pattern. Gordo's a pusher. Gordo goes to jail. The pen has a drug problem. Maybe Gordo's part of the problem, a cog in the mechanism of narcotics distribution. That would explain why Mrs. Gonzáles said everybody in La Pinta feared Ikie. Sure, he was in tight with the administration. So far, so good.

Tony Abeyta said Warden Jenks was suspected of trafficking at Germantown. But if Gonzáles and Jenks were working together, why would Jenks kill Gordo? That's where the whole thing collapses like a house of cards on an unmade bed. Oh, sure, thieves fall out, as they say, and so do drug dealers. Turf wars happen all the time on the streets. But in the pen, a closed little world like some kind of biosphere, you can't introduce any germs without everybody sneezing. There's no way Gordo could have taken over distribution without Jenks' okay. He needed the warden, but the warden didn't need him. Plenty of other mules in his stable. Still, why waste the man? What kind of threat did he represent? That must be it. Some kind of threat. And how did Baekke fit into this? Maybe he didn't. She felt she had some pieces of the puzzle, but not all of them.

"Matty!" Dodi suddenly cried. She was staring at a woman on crutches slowly hobbling out the door. "I just remembered! Herbie's message. He said, 'The gimp says get off this case.' The gimp…"

"Marcus Penner!" Slipping into her chair, Gloria beat Matty to the punch.

Rita's eyes were huge. "Penner! Warden talked about him. That phone call I sorta accidentally overheard, I told you. He said Penner told David Reese you'd talked to Glo."

Gloria looked as if she was going to be sick again. To distract her, Matty said the first thing that popped into her head. "How come Penner limps, Gloria? Polio or something like that?"

Gloria found her voice with difficulty. "Back when he was a kid in Kansas City, there was this other gang, and they thought he was working their territory. They kneecapped him. That was way back before so many kids had Uzi's and stuff."

"Jesus!"

Rita said she'd better take Glo home. Reluctantly, Dwight escorted them out the door.

Dodi began to gather up her things.

"Dodi, did you say you haven't filed suit yet?"

"No, we've got two years to file a complaint. I sent a Notice of Intent as soon as I talked to Mrs. Gonzáles. I know she's hot to trot, but…"

"No, no. You take your time. Take all the time you need."

Matty slept until 10:00. She spent the rest of the day cramming for an exam. She'd missed class on Wednesday, but the instructor scheduled a make-up Friday morning. Fat lot of good that would do if Matty didn't study. Only four weeks into the semester, and she was already behind.

There was a check in the mail from Al Montana. She figured she'd take a break and give the man a call.

"Hey, thanks for the money, Al."

"Matty, baby, you won't believe what Debbie's gone and done to me now!"

She waited impatiently until he paused to catch his breath. "¡Qué lástima! Listen, Al…"

"What am I gonna tell ya."

"You know anything about Doomsday Machine? It's a group, Doomsday Machine, and Marcus Penner, I think he's their manager or something."

"Penner? Bad news, baby, like the Cowboys losing in O. T."

"Tell me about him."

"You kidding, Matty? The secret of a long and happy life: avoid fatty foods and Marcus Penner. Good fellas like him…"

"Penner's in the mob?"

"Well, maybe. I dunno for a fact, but I do know he's into dealing. Uses the band as a front. Leastways, that's the word on the street. The band members, they're trippin' on eighth notes, I don't think any of them are involved, but you know what they say, 'Life is short, but art endures.'"

Al was full of surprises.

Friday morning, Matty somehow passed the psych exam. She was having second thoughts about an AAS in Criminal Justice. Sometimes Matty suspected she already knew more about the criminal justice system than most of the denizens of ivory towerdom.

All at once, she remembered a civil suit she'd sat in on, something to do with Corrections. She'd been trying to think of it since she met Dodi. She'd thought it was one of her own cases, but she was wrong. As a sheriff's deputy, she'd been detailed to guard the plaintiff, Jerry Manzanares, an inmate at the pen. Manzanares had been beaten by a gang of *vatos* out for a good time.

The state paraded half a dozen Ph.D.'s with graphs and flow charts. The plaintiff countered with a single expert witness. Asked about security at the pen, the former warden at Angola testified, "That ain't the way I'd have done it." The jury found for the plaintiff in the amount of $250,000. Not bad, considering Manzanares was his own attorney. At least, he didn't have to split the fee.

Matty wore black to class. She had to go directly from campus to Willie Nhung's funeral. After the service, everybody was invited to the parish hall for eats, the "funeral meats," Matty reminded herself.

She spotted Gilbert Gurulé hovering over the coffee pot like a bee in a bed of geraniums. Matty hesitated. Here was a golden opportunity to buttonhole the Secretary of Corrections, but it "wasn't the done thing," as Rodney would say, to talk business at a funeral. Matty didn't care what people thought, but she didn't want to hurt Carolyn's feelings.

Almost as if she had read Matty's mind, Carolyn came up to her and gave her a hug. "Go ahead, Matty," she said, nodding in the secretary's direction. "Okay."

"Mr. Secretary." He turned to her and smiled. "My name's Matty Madrid, and I'm investigating the death of Gordo Gonzáles."

"I wouldn't care to comment on that. Since the matter is in litigation—"

"How do you know it's in litigation? Sure! Gloria tells the gimp, and he tells Corrections. Shit!"

"A regrettable accident," Gurulé said sadly.

"What if it wasn't an accident? I've received information that three inmates murdered Gonzáles in cold blood, Foster, Gallegos, and Ruiz. And now the three of them are dead, too. What about that?"

"Young lady, you must understand that prisons are inherently dangerous places."

"Don't you see? Don't you understand? It was a set-up. Gordo was set up and so were the others." She was angry. "And night before last, I got an anonymous phone call threatening my life just minutes after somebody unloaded a twelve-gauge into my living room!"

Gilbert Gurulé shook his head. "If the legislature would only appropriate the monies needed for the construction of new prisons, we could more readily address the serious social problems confronting our fair state."

"You haven't listened to a thing I've been saying."

"Let me assure you that this administration will do its utmost to lead the people of New Mexico into the twenty-first century with absolute dedication and utmost compassion." The smile with which Secretary Gurulé had greeted Matty never left his handsome face. It was like talking to a bowl of bread pudding, only Gran's *capirotada* had more character than Gilbert Gurulé.

Matty forgot about Ira Walz and his busloads of protestors until she attempted to drive down Old Santa Fe Trail on her way to Dodi's office on San Francisco Street. She wanted to ask Dodi if she'd talked to Gordo's mother. But streams of demonstrators flowed across the street like the Rio Grande in springtime. Oblivious to traffic and public opinion, they flooded the capitol grounds.

Some in the crowd were chanting, "Bissel lives! Bissel lives!" They wore T-shirts featuring an electric chair in a circle with a line dividing the circle diagonally. But nobody's ever been electrocuted in this state, Matty told herself. An electric chair's been sitting unused in the basement of the Main Facility for thirty years, only now we gotta inject them lethally.

The demonstrators carried placards and banners, "THOU SHALT NOT KILL" and "CAPITAL PUNISHMENT = CAPITOL MURDER." The signs were, to use an unfortunate choice of words, executed professionally.

That surprised Matty. She'd been at the Federal Building when Navajo uranium miners from Cibola County protested long-term exposure to radioactivity. She'd been moved by the plethora of home-made signs. Some were misspelled; on others the words were scrunched together. But each was imprinted with its maker's tears.

This was altogether different. "Slick, Walz," she muttered. "Pretty slick."

Speaking of the King of Rome....

Ira Walz opened the door of the Toyota on the passenger's side and hopped in. "What the…"

Somebody honked. The stream of protestors had slowed to a trickle, allowing traffic to inch forward. Matty thought she'd better move. Santa Fe drivers speed and cut you off, never use their turn signals, and drink to excess, but they hardly ever lay on their horns. When they do, you'd better pay attention.

"What the hell's going on?"

"I thought it was you! Well, any port in a storm. Ha, ha! Listen, I need a ride up to Fort Marcy Park."

"Fort Marcy!"

"Hey, hey. It's just up there. You go through the town square and head north."

"I know where it is," she snapped, "and it's a plaza, not a square. What do you think this is, Boston? You want to go to Fort Marcy, fine. You take a taxi. Now, *chu*!"

Walz made no move to go. "They let us camp at the park. Isn't that cool? Only I forgot my notes. I'm making a speech, kind of a keynote address. Hurry it up, will you? Everybody's waiting."

Matty felt a pang of envy for James Bond's Aston Martin, the one with an ejection seat on the passenger's side. She came to a full stop in the middle of an intersection. A battered black truck stopped behind her.

Walz didn't get out, but somebody else got in. A little man with a big gun pointed it at Matty's head. His hand shook.

"Hey, good buddy," Walz said, "you want this bucket of bolts, you go right ahead, only let me out, okay?"

"*¡Hijo!* Who you calling a bucket of bolts!" Matty shrieked.

"Shut up, the both of you," the man with the gun demanded. "You, lady, turn this heap around and keep goin'." He waved the gun in the air. "We're goin' fer a little ride, jus' the three of us."

All she could think about were the gratuitous insults splattering the Red Menace like spring rain. Seething at Walz, the carjacker, and Lucius Bissel, who'd inadvertently brought them all together, Matty drove south to I-25. Maybe she'd get Dodi to sue Bissel. She'd heard about corrections workers in France or someplace suing inmates over bad working conditions. The workers argued they wouldn't have to put in overtime if the inmates had obeyed the law of the land in the first place.

When they reached the Interstate, the carjacker directed her to drive north, towards Denver. Walz tried to reason with him until the little man threatened to use the New Yorker's brains to polish the upholstery.

Matty drove erratically, hoping to attract the attention of a Smokey. Unfortunately, her driving wasn't noticeably worse than anybody else's on New Mexico's highways. A tourist from Indiana crept along at sixty-five or seventy. Matty passed him as if he were standing still. Glancing in the rear view mirror, she spotted the battered black truck which had followed them from downtown Santa Fe. Matty didn't believe in coincidence.

When the little man with the large gun ordered Matty to exit the highway at Goose Neck, she knew this was no random carjacking. Following his directions, she drove past the turnoff to the Gonzáles' adobe and headed into the mountains until they came to a log cabin, a line shack, maybe, or the fragment of a homesteader's broken dream.

The black truck pulled up behind them. A tall, skinny man in black got out. Matty recognized the preacher, Ordell Koonz. She'd met him at Erlene's house on her second, scary visit when Sonny put the moves on her.

The carjacker ordered them out. "Here they is, Preacher!"

"Partch! You stupid fool!" Koonz knocked him to the ground. "I told you to blindfold 'er! Tie 'er up an' blindfold 'er."

Partch struggled to get up. "It weren't my fault! They was two of 'em. You never tol' me they was two of 'em. I needed the girl to drive. It weren't never my fault!"

"Shut up! Get 'em in the cabin and keep your gun on 'em. You think you can do that awright?"

Whimpering like a dog that's been kicked by its cruel master, Partch waved Walz and Matty inside. Matty thought about jumping the little man when he came in the door, but she figured Walz would only mess everything up. Walz was very quiet. Maybe the kidnappers had scared him. They certainly scared Matty. Matty Madrid, who could handle anything and anybody, suddenly wanted to hurry home to Esperanza. She didn't want to be here, that was for sure.

The cabin was unfit for human habitation. Half the roof had collapsed within, and the wind blew through the chinks in the walls. Several folding chairs marked "Property NMHU Do Not Remove" were scattered in a semi-circle around a large cardboard box. A Bible rested on top of the box. Behind the makeshift pulpit, a crudely lettered sign proclaimed "The Church of the Righteous Sword and Shield."

"Sit down!" Koonz thundered. They sat down quickly like little kids playing musical chairs. The preacher ordered Partch to keep an eye on them while he handcuffed each of them to a chair.

"That lawyer lady called Erlene Gonzáles," he said to Matty. "She says mebbe hit ain't no accident Gordo's goin' to glory."

"Listen…"

"No, you listen to me, missy. That money was goin' to be my money. My money! To build a rock of salvation in this quicksand of papish idolatry!" Matty found herself wondering how anybody could build a rock except maybe God and Old Father Time. "We wuz goin' to make two million, five million bucks off o' him passin'!"

The hell you were, Matty said to herself. *The Tort Claims Act won't allow the state to be liable for that much money. Dodi Koren told me so. Multimillion dollar damage awards are about as likely as Big Foot's fathering a space alien's twins in Graceland's parking lot.* "Five million bucks! Enough to buy this mountain and build a new Jerusalem upon it."

"Amen!" Partch shouted.

Matty couldn't contain herself any longer. "What the hell are you talking about?"

The preacher's eyes glowed like a cat's. "Doom is coming on this present age. Only 144,000 will be saved, the Good Book says, men and women as white as the snow, pure in chastity, humility and Godly love."

"We wuz gonna buy this here mountain," Partch said, more succinctly if somewhat less inspired.

Koonz continued as if he hadn't heard him. "For five million dollars, we could buy this mountain and build us a permanent compound. We can train the soldiers of the Righteous Sword and Shield to gird themselves in readiness for the millennium. 'There was a war in heaven. Michael and his angels…'"

"You're nuts!" Ira Walz blurted out. "Totally bananas!"

Koonz struck him repeatedly until Walz gagged on his own blood.

"The devil in America prowls like a roaring lion, devouring the sinner. And you," he leaned over Matty until his spittle spattered her face, "you, Matty Madrid, you are an agent of the antichrist. If Erlene's suit is thrown out of the court…"

"Wait a minute. You don't understand. It won't be thrown out. If I'm right and Gordo was murdered, Mrs. Gonzáles can still sue Corrections. But it's a federal case now, it's constitutional, and that means no cap on the damages. You're sitting pretty, Preacher. All you gotta do is wait."

Ordell Koonz stopped his raving. "All right, missy," he said. "We'll jes' see 'bout that. But I figger a little persuasion might be in order. I'm goin' keep y'all here till we gits the cash."

Matty and Walz began speaking at once.

"What? You can't…"

"…as a fruitcake!"

"Listen," Matty argued. "It'll be months before this case comes up, and then there's appeals and it'll take years!"

Koonz sneered. "Then, y'all better make yerself comf'table. You're goin' to be here a mighty long time." He jerked his head in the direction of the front door, and he and Partch left together.

"What the hell…"

"Shhh!" Matty listened for the sound of a key turning in the lock. She heard a vehicle start up and drive away. It sounded like a truck, but it wasn't the Red Menace. She knew its wheezes, coughs, and rattles as a mother knows her baby's cry.

"I'm going back to Long Island," Walz said. "It's safer in New York. Sheesh!"

"Shut up, will you?" Matty snapped. "I gotta think. We gotta get out of here. These cuffs…"

"Come over here."

"What?"

"Wiggle your chair until you get close enough to reach inside my jacket," Walz directed. "There's a tube of Vaseline in the inside pocket."

"*Vaseline?*"

"Rub it on your wrists, so you can slip out of the handcuffs."

Matty was flabbergasted, but she did as she was told. "How the hell…"

"Hey, hey! I get arrested all the time. Sometimes it come in handy, like when you need your hands free to defend yourself from the drunks in a holding tank."

After a few minutes, Matty slipped out of Koonz' handcuffs. She rubbed Walz' wrists with Vaseline until he was able to do the same. Rushing to the cabin door, they found it locked just as Matty had feared.

"Stand back," she ordered. Flinging herself at the door, she kicked it open with both feet. She ripped her black knit skirt, but she didn't stop to worry about it. She'd add it to Erlene's bill under "Miscellaneous Expenses." They ran to the Toyota and jumped in. The keys were in the ignition, and Matty's purse lay on the floor. She picked up the Browning and checked to see if it was loaded. Holding it in her right hand, she sped down the mountain like a kid on a Flexible Flyer.

When she reached the Interstate, she headed south. "Shouldn't we tell somebody what happened?" Walz asked, looking with longing at the arrow pointing north towards Las Vegas.

"I'm gonna tell the sheriff of Santa Fe County," Matty said. "I don't know anybody in the San Miguel S. O., and we're kinda parochial about our crimes. That's why I didn't tell anybody about Sonny … You've got to admit, it sounds pretty *loco*. They might put us in the nuthouse instead. It's so damn convenient."

"Huh?"

"The state mental hospital is up in Las Vegas." She giggled. "Only now they wanna call it the Center for Gerontology and Psychiatry." She giggled again. Some kind of delayed reaction setting in, she figured. Don't lose it, she told herself. You're almost home free. Home at last. Home to Gran and Esperanza.

Bee, bee, bumblebee.
All out, come in free.

Friday afternoon, Lucius Bissel was moved from his cell block in the max unit to the death house, a concrete cubicle standing by itself inside the triple razor wire that distinguishes the North Facility from less restricted houses of correction.

Bissel laughed and joked with the extraction team. "Well, lookie here," he said. "The movin' men done showed up at last. Tell y' what. Let's head on down to Mexico, boys. Have us a good ol' time."

The CO's kept their mouths shut. Nobody on the extraction team liked Bissel. He hadn't gotten any write-ups, and he hadn't gone *loco*, bouncing off the walls in Unit 3, the way some of them do. But they all knew what he was in for, the brutal rape and murder of a fifteen-year-old girl. Each male officer was somebody's husband or father, brother or son. Bissel's victim could have been a loved one of his own. The only woman on the team figured it was the luck of the draw she wasn't the victim of a callous predator like Bissel. She resented the legal apparatus that allows a convicted killer to go on living at the taxpayers' expense long after his victim was food for worms.

Warden Jenks came by to see him shortly after Bissel had settled into sleeping quarters next to the Capital Punishment Room. There, the condemned man would be strapped onto a stainless steel table while a lethal injection was administered through a rubber tube with all the irrefutable logic of gravity. Bissel's "last mile" was only a few yards long.

"Well, now, Lucius," Jenks said. "Looks like we ain't goin' to have the pleasure of yer comp'ny here much longer."

"Don't you be too sure of that, Warden," Bissel said with a lopsided grin. "Maybe the governor's gonna set aside m' sentence, write me a reprieve, maybe even a pardon. Maybe he'll extradite me to Vietnam, like that lawyer fella promised 'em up in Attica, or, hell, even Cuba. Son of a bitch owes me a favor anyhow."

"Favor? You?"

"Yeah. Hell, I was gonna vote for him once. Figgered he was the lesser of two evils, and dogged if I wasn't right."

Jenks chuckled. "Don't you get yer hopes up. Seems to me you're gonna meet yer maker quicker 'n you can say 'Jackie Robinson.'"

"You're a liar, Jenks. My maker? You figger me meetin' up with the devil tomorrow, and you know it. Well, I'll be sure to let him know you're comin'. Lemme tell you somethin', Harley. Only diff'rence 'tween you an' me is I got caught."

"Watch yer mouth, you asshole!" Jenks snarled.

"What you gonna do to me? Gimme a write-up? Put me in lockdown? Listen, you sonofabitch. You can kill me, but you can't shut me up. I'm gonna come back an' haunt you, Harley Jenks. Back from the grave," he intoned sepulchrally.

"Oh, fer..." Warden Jenks turned to go.

"Whooooooo!" Bissel fell back on his bunk. He was laughing too hard to stand up.

Matty dropped Walz off at the Roundhouse too late to deliver his keynote address, she noted with satisfaction. Pouring back onto the buses, the demonstrators were ready to roll to the penitentiary. They planned to protest until Bissel was executed at midnight or the governor granted him clemency, whichever came first. Since the governor didn't show mercy to families below the poverty line and sick folks with five-figure hospital bills, Matty figured he wasn't likely to have any pity left over for the likes of Lucius Bissel. Still, in an election year, you never know. Granting clemency would win him the votes of both inmates on death row. Of course, convicted felons lose the right to vote, but that doesn't matter much in New Mexico. People who've been dead and buried ten or twenty years have been known to vote in recent elections, especially in Santa Catalina County. Nice to know the spirits are so civic-minded.

She zipped over to the County Law Complex to which the sheriff's office had moved a few months ago. At least, she figured, you could find a place to park at the complex. Sheriff Maes listened to Matty's story in silence. He entered the name of Ordell Koonz into his computer by hunting and pecking. "Hmph," he grunted.

"Hmph... what?"

"Your friend Koonz has got hisself a record. Buncha his people beat up a man and his wife in Raton, only his goons ratted on him to save themselves some jail time. Said he put 'em up to it. Seems the couple was tryin' to opt out of the Church of the...whazzat?"

"Righteous Sword and Shield. Maybe you need glasses, Sheriff."

"Kid like me?" The sheriff scowled. "It's the itty-bitty type they use on these damn things. Gets smaller ever' year. Mr. and Mrs. ..." He squinted at the screen. "...Ortega claim they was fleeced outta five thousand bucks by Ordell Koontz and his followers. When they changed their minds and decided to join the Assembly of God instead, Koonz unleashed his muscle on 'em."

"He do any time?"

The sheriff nodded. "Got him on aggravated battery. Larceny charges wouldn't stick. He got a passle of receipts and tax records, all nice and legal. You go over to San Gerónimo's and you pop some money in the poor box, you can't holler 'Fraud!' just 'cause St. Jude don't find your lost canary. Leastways, that's how the grand jury seen it."

"I'll give Trini Gabaldón over in Las Vegas a call, but I got a awful feeling he ain't gonna be able to do nothin' 'bout it. Your word against him and this other fella, and him bein' a preacher an' all."

"But the handcuffs, the chairs..."

The sheriff shook his head. "Smart cookie like Koonz is gonna wiggle out of it. He'll hide the evidence or else he'll claim you planted it. Tryin' to get him outta the picture so's you could muscle in on Erlene's millions."

"Bull!"

"Fact is, I suspect that's what he's doin' right now, settin' up his story 'fore Sheriff Gabaldón gets there. Why don't you go on home. Rearrange your closets or somethin'. Let the big boys handle this. Tell you what. Why don't you go shoppin'? Buy yourself somethin' pretty. Maybe a new outfit. That one you got on's kinda tore. Mervyn's havin' a big sale on ladies' dresses. My wife and her sister's plannin' on makin' a day of it." The sheriff sighed deeply.

As soon as Ordell Koonz saw the splintered door, he knew what had happened. He buried the handcuffs in the woods. Directing Partch to clean up the Vaseline and to sponge the episode from his mind, Koonz went into Goose Neck to see Erlene.

"Preacher!" Her face lit up when she saw him. Inwardly, Koonz groaned. He'd hoped to parlay Erlene's infatuation into easy money. On the whole, he'd rather service a sow in heat than Erlene Gonzáles ever again.

"They got away." He sat down beside her.

"They what?"

"They got clean away."

Erlene was so besotted with the preacher, she couldn't bring herself to snap at him. Instead, she yelled at the only other person in the room. "Hardhead!"

"Momma?"

"What you lookin' at? Swear you're as google-eyed as a hop toad."

"Momma!"

"Go kill me somethin' fer supper. Go on. Git!"

Cradling the Winchester in his arms, Sonny departed, leaving Erlene and Koonz alone.

The preacher cleared his throat. "Sister, she's like to have the sheriff on our necks. You got to make your Bible oath you'll say nothin' 'bout any of this. You kin tell 'em 'bout the lawsuit. That's okay, but if they ask you what you're goin' to do with the money, tell 'em you jes' want to provide fer yer ol' age. Yup." He nodded, pleased with his ingenuity. "You lost yer boy, and you gotta provide somehow fer yer ol' age."

Mrs. Gonzáles was nettled. She liked to tell herself she didn't look a day over forty. "Swear to God, Preacher, I won't say nothin'. They ain't never gonna know nothin'. You kin count on me. You know you kin allus count on me, Ordell." She put her arms around him.

Koonz shot up like a sky rocket. "I gotta git on back up the mountain. I don't trust that fool Partch to git the job done right."

Erlene's face fell. "But, Preacher, We're all alone here. Sonny won't be back fer hours. Ain't nobody to see," she murmured. With a massive effort, she hauled herself off the couch. Pressing her body against Koonz', she whispered, "Ain't nobody here but us'n."

The preacher shoved her aside. "Gotta be goin'," he muttered and ran out the open door.

Alone in the tumble-down adobe, Erlene Gonzáles howled like a soul in Hell.

Friday evening, a CO brought Lucius Bissel dinner in a styrofoam container: a slice of canned ham, some veggies, and a cup of mixed fruit for dessert.

"What the hell's this?"

"That's your supper, Bissel," the officer replied. "Eat hearty."

"I didn't order this."

"¡Oh, chiste! You think I'm room service or somethin'?"

"Nah, I ordered me a steak, well done, an' some o' them French fries an' beans, and a bottle of wine, not too sweet." He smacked his lips.

"Bissel, you somethin' else!"

At eleven o'clock, the chaplain looked in on him. "Hello, *Pa-*

dre," Bissel said. "You want somebody for yourall's Friday night bingo? 'Fraid I'm all tied up."

"Thought you might like some company, Lucius."

"Don't you gimme none of that crap!" Bissel snarled. "You want me to fall down on my knees and repent. 'Hallelujah, Jesus!' Ain't that it? Ain't it?"

The chaplain sighed. After eleven years at the pen, the vagaries of human nature failed to surprise him. They didn't even depress him any more, but his feet hurt. He wondered what it was like to go home at 5:00, to put your feet up and relax with a beer and a ball game on TV. "I want everybody on their knees, my son, if it helps them draw near to God. Without a miracle, I'm not going to get it, but I believe in miracles. It's part of the job description. I just thought you might like to talk."

"I got nothin' to say, *Padre.* I done what I done, and I ain't sayin' I'm sorry to nobody. I'm goin' do my time in hell is all."

They stood in silence until Bissel asked the chaplain, "You go fishin' when you was on vacation like you's gonna?"

The chaplain smiled. "I went up to Navajo Lake. Caught a real nice mess of brownies."

They talked about fishing until the extraction team came to escort the condemned man into the next room.

It was after visiting hours at the South Facility, so Matty telephoned Mingo's caseworker, asking to speak with him. "It's a family emergency," she said, neglecting to mention it was Gordo's family that had created the emergency.

After about an hour and a half, Mingo returned her call. "Matty, honey. *¿Qué pasa,* babe?"

"Mingo! You're not going to believe this…"

"Honey, I believe everything you tell me. Keeps me warm on

long winter nights."

"Mingo, I got kidnapped."

"What?"

"Guy named Ordell Koonz. Calls himself 'the preacher'. Sheriff Maes says he's been in the joint. You know him?"

"Preacher? Yeah, I know 'im. Sure, I know the preacher." He let out a low whistle. "In here for beatin' a guy up and his wife."

"I know all about that. Tell me something I don't know."

Mingo lowered his voice. "He's a brother, big cheese in the AB. You don' wanna mess with them."

"The AB?"

"The Brotherhood, the Aryan Brotherhood. Only Koonz got too *loco* for 'em, and they kicked 'em out. Wants to build a kingdom on a mountain top somewheres for all the elect, all of 'em white. Meantime, the rest of us is gonna burn, blacks and browns and reds and yellas."

"What do you mean? Burn in hell? Some kind of divine judgment?"

"Revolution. Like in Los Angeles. The race of Ham is gonna rise up against the oppressor, an' they're gonna kill 'em, an' then they're gonna kill each other off, an' the rest of us, what Koonz calls the mongrel nations. Preacher and his followers be the only ones left. Come the millennium, they'll march right into heaven with plenty of elbow room to spare."

"The millennium. Remind me to put it on my calendar."

"Yeah. Y' oughtta hear him go on about it. You hear it once, you never gonna forget it. Man's on the level, 'cept it ain't enough to get everybody ready for the comin' rain of blood. He wants to start it, preachin' revolution."

"Jesus!"

"And the Church of the Righteous Sword and Shield's gonna sit back on its mountain top an' laugh."

"The New Jerusalem."

"Whatever."

"Okay, you've been a big help. Thanks."

"You comin' tomorrow? Maybe I can find you out some more."

"I don't know if I'm coming or going, much less where. We'll have to see. Okay?"

"I read you."

"*Bueno*, bye."

Lucius Bissel's last words were, "Mama, I'm comin' home." Death penalty opponents declared themselves deeply touched by his dying words. But an enterprising reporter on the *Journal North* discovered Bissel's mother had abandoned him and his baby sister in a Tucumcari bus station in 1952. Mama's present whereabouts were unknown. Since then, Bissel had formed no relationship with any woman lasting more than twenty minutes. The reporter concluded that Bissel's farewell to life was in keeping with the rest of it, thumbing his nose at everything and everybody. *Tal vida, tal muerte:* Such a life, such a death. But she was paid to report the news and not to opine, so she kept her conclusions to herself.

At six minutes after midnight, Dr. Delattre pronounced Inmate Bissel "dead as a doornail."

Ira Walz and the Coalition to Stop Senseless Violence piled back on the buses and headed east, singing "Ninety-nine Bottles of Beer on the Wall." By the time the sun came up, they were well on their way to El Reno, Oklahoma, where a double execution was scheduled the following Wednesday.

In Pie Town, the parents of Bissel's victim clung to each other through the night. Weeping would have brought a welcome measure of relief, but twelve years after their daughter's murder, they had no more tears to shed.

(HAPTER SIX

Saturday morning, Matty stopped by the County Law Complex. "Matty!" the sheriff barked at her. "Matty dear, you reckon you could take dictation?"

"What's up?" she asked.

Leroy Maes stuck a pad and pencil in her hand and motioned for her to follow. "Bernalillo County sent us up a suspect last night, and I'm 'bout to interrogate 'im. Ain't nobody 'round on a Saturday to take his statement."

"Sheriff, you know I've assisted in interrogations before."

Maes came to a full stop. "Jus' keep your mouth shut, pretty please. Promise me that."

"You know what they say." Matty grinned. "'Flies don't go in a mouth that's shut.'"

The sheriff snorted as he opened the door to the interrogation room. The suspect was a pasty-faced man, about forty. His eyes darted from the sheriff to Matty and then to Gus, who was leaning against the wall, his arms folded across his chest. Gus looked for all the world like a horse player who just played a long shot and lost.

Straddling a straight-back chair, Sheriff Maes sat down at the table. "Your name is Arthur Henley Guy," he said.

"Yeah, okay, that's me."

Matty began to scribble. Out of the corner of her eye, she saw Gus activate the tape recorder. With a taped transcript, a verbatim statement, and three witnesses, Guy wouldn't be able to weasel out of a confession. She wondered if he'd been Mirandized yet. Maes would probably get around to it sooner or later.

"Arthur Guy… only they call you 'the Dodger'. How come?"

Guy shrugged. "Fella in the joint, 'the Professor.' He said I was kinda like the Artful Dodger 'count of 'cause I was always gettin' outta scrapes. Know what I mean?"

"'Artful'… who?"

"Some guy in a movie. I dunno." He shrugged again. "Maybe it was on the TV. Some baseball player I s'pose. Los Angeleez."

The sheriff took his time studying the papers on the desk in front of him. He rubbed his nose. "Looks like you ain't too awful artful, Mr. Guy. Says here you was doin' time for murder."

"Yeah, okay." Guy wriggled like a snake shedding its skin. "I paid my debit to society. They gimme parole."

"So it says, Mr. Guy. You got your sentence reduced by half 'cause of Good Time. Ain't that nice. And, lookey here, warden himself give the parole board a testimonial to your sterling character."

"I kept my nose clean," Guy said, staring at the door with unbridled longing.

"The operative word is 'kept,' Mr. Guy." The sheriff's wisp of a smile faded like morning mist. "'Kept' your nose clean. Maybe you got the sniffles." Maes reached for a box of Kleenex on the table and shoved it in front of Arthur Guy. Guy stared at it in horror.

"Where was you on Wednesday night, Mr. Guy?" the sheriff asked quietly.

"Lemme see." Guy shook his head. "I don't remember."

"Three nights ago and you don't remember?"

Guy bit his lip. "Okay, uh, I was out drinkin'. Yeah, I was on a tear, drinkin' all night. Yeah."

"Izzat a fact? And where was it you was on this here tear, Mr.

Guy?"

"Some bar." Guy fidgeted in his seat. Gus rested his hands on the back of the chair. Guy glanced at the deputy and sat still.

"And what was the name of this establishment?"

"Some bar. I dunno." Pleased with himself, Guy suddenly grinned.

"It's a damn funny thing, Mr. Guy, but we got us rules in New Mexico. A felon, he's on parole, he goes into a bar, he's violatin' the conditions of his parole. He can go back to the joint. Ain't that a funny thing."

"I went to a movie. Yeah, I went to a movie. I got mixed up."

"Perfectly natural mistake, Mr. Guy. You got to the movie, you gonna see *Bambi* or somethin', and somehow you get the idea you're in a bar drinkin' intoxicatin' beverages. Happens all the time. My, my, my, my."

Guy didn't say anything.

"Well, now, here's the funny part, Arthur. You don't mind me callin' you 'Arthur'?" Guy stared at him. "We got a report you was dischargin' a loaded weapon into the residence of a Miss…"

The sheriff pretended to consult his notes, "Marta Madrid 'bout 10:00 Wednesday night. You wanna comment on that, Mr. Guy?"

"Wasn't me. No sir. I wasn't nowheres near Agua Fría, I tol' you I was in a movie over on—someplace."

The sheriff smiled. "Well, now, I would be real pleased to hear that, Arthur, 'cause it's also a violation of your parole to be a felon in possession of a deadly weapon. But we got us one little bitty problem."

Guy opened his mouth to speak, but nothing came out.

"How come you knowed she was on Agua Fría?" The sheriff suddenly stood up. "You fuckin' son of a bitch!" he roared. "You think I dunno you shot up Matty Madrid's place? Jesus Christ! There's a kid in there and a ol' lady, too. Jesus! You lucky I ain't bookin' you for murder. Lock 'im up, Ramírez!"

"No, hey, wait a minute." Guy was sweating profusely. "I didn't kill nobody. I didn't even try. You ask her. You ask the lady."

Matty bent her head over the notepad. Obviously, Guy hadn't put two and two together. If he did, they'd probably add up to five.

"Hell, I called her up after it was over. I jus' wanted to throw a scare in her." He wet his lips. "He tol' me to kill her, but I never, I ain't no stone killer, sheriff. It's true, like they say, I killed my wife's sister, but that wasn't my fault. She was askin' for it. Bitch never gimme no choice. But, Jeez, to kill somebody you don't even know… I saw her goin' to the hall, an' I figgered if I shot up the room a little when there wasn't nobody around, I could tell him I missed, is all. I swear it on my mother's grave!"

The sheriff sighed. "It says here your mother's livin' in Albuquerque. Says here she's a retired go-go dancer. Retired! What are they gonna do? Give 'er a gold watch and a testimonial dinner?"

"I never tried to kill that woman, Sheriff. Honest to God."

The sheriff sat down again. "So, you was gonna tell 'im you tried, only you missed."

Guy nodded.

"Who?"

"Jeez…"

"Who!"

"Salas. Deputy Warden Salas. He says if I don't help him, he'll get some dudes to say I was dealin', an' I never done drugs in my life. I never! I swear it on my mother's… I'm clean, sheriff, I tell ya."

"Yeah, like a baby's back side. Ramírez, get somebody in here to finish takin' this asshole's statement. Find out where he got the weapon."

"I picked it up in El Paso. Cost me three C-notes. Salas gimme the money. You go talk to Salas. He'll tell you."

"How come everybody's always tellin' me how to do my job?" The sheriff cast his eyes to heaven.

Guy cleared his throat nervously. "Salas called me last night.

Said I hadda finish the job. Said the bitch was talkin' to Gilbert Gurulé, and I hadda do somethin' about it. Said I could be doin' my parole in Unit 3." He shuddered.

"Ramírez, you and Jaramillo pick up Salas. I don't care if he's on penitentiary grounds. Hell, I don't care if he's tap dancin' at Sweeney Center. I want him in here.

"You." He looked at Matty and jerked his head. "Come with me."

Back in Maes' office, Matty asked him, "How did you get on to Guy?"

The sheriff snorted. "Punks like him never cover all the angles. I figgered he'd come runnin' home to mama, so I tipped Bernalillo County, and they picked him up for drunk and disorderly outside her apartment. Or maybe it was the home for elderly go-go dancers. I dunno."

"Good work, sheriff."

"Yeah, well, speakin' of good work, Matty, gotta give credit where credit's due, I s'pose." He sighed. "Report come back from Quantico."

"The gun!"

"Ten-four. They was able to raise the registration number, and you ain't never gonna guess who it was registered to. God bless the USA and Sarah Brady."

"Harley Jenks?"

He shook his head. "Deputy Warden Salas. So, you see, I wanna talk to Salas in a real bad way. I wanna talk to him so bad it hurts."

"Salas is Jenks' gopher."

"Well, that's as may be. Right now we ain't got nothin' on Jenks. If Salas was Jenks' gopher, like you say, he did a real good job 'cause all the signs point to him, and none of 'em points to his boss. I figger Salas is the key to this thing. But don't you worry your pretty little head none. Ramírez is goin' after Salas, and Ramírez is the best man I got, 'though God knows I'd never tell 'im. Give 'im a swell head. Ramírez'll brings Salas in, then we'll get crackin'.''

Contrary to the sheriff's expectations, his deputies did not bring Salas in for questioning Saturday morning. They arrived at the pen's Main Facility at 10:30. After cooling their heels forty-five minutes in the reception area, Gus asked to borrow the phone.

"Sheriff, this is Ramírez. I'm out here at the pen, and we're gettin' no cooperation from the folks here, so I figger if you wanna tell the governor to go ahead and send out the National Guard, that'll be okay."

He paused to listen to a recorded message announce the time and temperature. It was 11:14 and 62 degrees.

"That's a big ten-four. Me and Jaramillo'll secure reception. We'll hold 'em till you can get here."

The CO at reception promptly called his sergeant, who called a lieutenant, who radioed the watch commander, who suddenly came down with the twenty-four hour flu, leaving the chief of security to deal with the deputies. Major Olinger came into the reception area in less than two minutes. He stuck out his hand, but Gus ignored it. Gus wasn't much for the white man's quaint ethnic customs. He'd leave that up to the anthropologists. "Well now, boys," the major said. "What's all this about?"

"Police business, major," Gus said, stone-faced.

"Dwyer here says you're looking for the deputy warden." CO Dwyer slowly shrank out of sight behind the counter.

Gus nodded. "We'd just like to ask him a few questions."

"Maybe I can help you."

"We'd like to talk to the deputy warden."

"If you could just give me some idea…"

"Lemme put it this way. You gonna send Salas out or we gonna have to go in and get 'im?"

The COS threw up his hands. "He ain't here. Him and Reese

went hunting. They'll be back next week."

"Reese?"

"In-house counsel for the department."

Gus knew about Reese. Matty suspected Reese was involved with the Denver mob, and she'd shared her suspicions with the sheriff. "Where'd they go?"

"Hell, I don't know. Somewhere's up around San Antonio Mountain. I tell you I don't know."

"Who was drivin'?"

"Salas," Dwyer squeaked. He was expecting the National Guard to parachute into the yard at any moment and the president to declare the pen a national disaster. "He was drivin' his Land Cruiser. It's got a light bar on the top of it. Said it was fixin' to snow, and he'd need four-wheel drive."

Gus dashed to his vehicle. Jaramillo was right behind him. Thinking about Reese and Salas in the mountains with a couple of rifles and plenty of ammo made Gus a little nervous. He figured a bull elk wouldn't be the only trophy of that particular hunting expedition, and he didn't want San Antonio, the sacred mountain of the north, desecrated by violence. Not if he could help it. He directed dispatch to put out an APB on Salas' 4 x 4.

Back in reception, the COS glared at Dwyer.

"Look on the bright side, Major," the CO said. "At least, it wasn't no state car."

Major Olinger resolved to transfer Dwyer to morning watch where he'd have no further communication with civilians. Maybe Dwyer would like a transfer to Camp Sierra Blanca or even Timbuktu.

When Trinidad Gabaldón, Sheriff of San Miguel County, arrived at the Church of the Righteous Sword and Shield, he found a Sabbath Day service in full swing. Leroy Maes' phone call Friday had alerted the sheriff to Matty's abduction, but it took Gabaldón several hours to locate a judge and convince him to sign a warrant. Luckily, Judge Reyes, a lifelong member of Our Lady of Sorrows, didn't hold much truck with millennialists. Trini tracked him down at his daughter's house in Sapello. The judge was babysitting the twins while Corrine and her husband shopped for a new dishwasher.

"They did what? To who?"

The sheriff repeated what he'd told the judge twice already while he handed him the warrant and a ballpoint pen.

"*¡Jesús, María y José!*" the judge declared. "Bad enough when the Americans was after our land. Now they want to kick us out of heaven, too?"

A dozen people in the line shack were singing "Brother, Take the Hand of Jesus" when Trinidad Gabaldón arrived. He figured the congregation probably wasn't much into gender inclusiveness. Trini read everything printed in the Las Vegas *Optic* about religion, so he knew all about gender inclusive hymnody.

When he was at West Las Vegas High, he'd thought about becoming a Franciscan, but that was before Mary Anne Sedillo told him she was pregnant. One wedding and seven kids later, Trini figured it had all been for the best. As sheriff of San Miguel County, he wrestled with the devil as often as any priest. He had seen the hand of God writing boldly upon the affairs of men. Sometimes His handwriting was a little hard to read.

The singing petered out as the sheriff and his deputies fanned out inside the church.

"Mr. Koonz…"

"*Brother* Koonz." The preacher rolled his shirtsleeves down and buttoned the cuffs. He'd taken his jacket off. Bible-thumping is mighty hot work.

"This here's a warrant empowering us to search the premises." The sheriff looked about him, making no effort to hide his distaste. "Why don't you send these folks back home, only I'm gonna have to ask you and Mr. Partch to stay put."

Gabaldón expected the preacher to object, spouting scripture like a whale spouts water, but Koonz nodded at Partch, who dismissed the congregation with the pious admonition to "walk in the light." Trini noted with relief that Erlene Gonzáles and her son were not in the line shack. He sometimes joked that a room in the county jail was permanently reserved under Sonny's name on Saturday nights.

Gabaldón directed one of his deputies, Angel Serrano, to keep an eye on the suspects while the rest of the team searched the cabin. It was Serrano's first opportunity to investigate anything bigger than a fender bender on Highway 65, but Trini wanted more experienced officers conducting the search. The kid still had a lot to learn.

"Hey, Sheriff, look at this."

The sheriff went over to see what his deputy had found, a cardboard box stuffed with tracts. "Would you look at that? 'God is a White American.' Gee, I never knew that."

His curiosity piqued, Deputy Serrano glanced in their direction. At that moment, Sonny Gonzáles barrelled through the front door. He held the Winchester in both hands and before Angel Serrano could turn around, Sonny fired twice, hitting Serrano and Gabaldón.

The sheriff was vaguely aware of his deputies exchanging shots with Sonny, but the flashes of gunfire hurt his eyes, and he turned his head. He saw Angel Serrano on the dirt floor, bleeding from a wound in his neck. The deputy's eyes were fixed on the hole in the ceiling. Maybe he was looking into eternity. The sheriff wondered what it looked like.

Gabaldón felt oddly detached from the noise and confusion. Maybe dying is like that, gradually distancing yourself from the world around you, sailing out to sea, friends and loved ones on the shore. His brother-in-law joined the Merchant Marine in 1987. *Brother, take the hand of Jesus.*

He forced himself to think about his wife. He wanted to see Mary Anne again. He wanted to remind her little Rudy's bike was on layaway at Sears. She'd have to make the payments every week until December 23. Every week, Mary Anne. Don't you forget.

The judge's daughter was shopping for a dishwasher. Maybe she shopped at Sears. Somehow, it seemed important to tell Corrine to get a Maytag. A Maytag, Corrine. You get a Maytag. A Maytag lasts and lasts. Like eternity, only a dishwasher runs in shorter cycles.

When the shooting stopped, the shack was silent except for Pearl Partch crying, "I been shot! Oh, Lordy, I been shot. Help me. I'm a-gonna die!" One of Gabaldón's deputies crept out of hiding. He saw Partch writhing on the floor, but there was no sign of Sonny Gonzáles or Ordell Koonz. Sheriff Gabaldón was alive, but unconscious. When he looked into Angel Serrano's vacant eyes, the deputy crossed himself. Reaching inside his shirt, he fingered the scapular his mother always made him wear.

"Rick?" He called out to the other deputy. He was surprised at the sound of his voice. It quavered like an old woman's. "Rick! You there?"

Rick crept out from behind the makeshift pulpit. "Jesus God!" he said.

"See what you can do for the sheriff. I gotta get on the radio. We're gonna need help."

"Angel! God…"

"Look after the sheriff, Rick! Trini's been hit." He peered through the open door, but nobody was there. He wished the woods surrounding the cabin were out of rifle range. His service revolver would be useless if somebody was in the woods with a .22.

Darting from side to side, the deputy reached the sheriff's Blazer. Shielding himself behind the body of the vehicle, he managed to raise dispatch. When at last he signed off, he discovered he was crying.

"So, you got everything?"

Glo looked around. The furnishings, which she'd rented along with the duplex for $525 a month, were all in place. Everything else had been packed into her van. "Yeah, okay, Rita, that's it."

"You call me when you get to Peñasco, okay?"

Glo nodded. "It'll be okay. I'm just gonna spend the weekend, unload my stuff, you know?"

"And Monday…"

"Monday I check into the rehab center in Taos. It'll be okay. I promise."

"I don't want you worrying about none of this shit out there at the pen."

"I'm gonna testify, they ask me. I gave 'em a statement already. It's like, I kinda owe it to Mac. You know?"

Rita gave her a hug. "I know. But don't you worry about a thing, honey. It's all gonna be okay. You'll see. It'll be okay."

Responding to San Miguel County's 10-61, an alert DPS officer stopped to question a woman sitting by the side of the road leading from Goose Neck into the mountains. She was sobbing uncontrollably. She admitted she'd been among the members of the congregation who met Sonny Gonzáles on his way to church. They'd told him about armed men breaking into the line shack.

"It's coming!" he'd shouted. "Direful day of doom!" Shouldering his rifle, he ran off in the direction of the church.

The state police quickly cordoned off the road. They figured Sonny and the preacher were on foot. The alternator on the preacher's truck was broken. He'd told Partch to fix it, but Partch forgot. And Sonny's momma wouldn't let him drive. The last time he drove her Ford Fairlane to Las Vegas, he'd managed to scrap both sides at once squeezing into a parking space reserved for a motorcycle. He'd hitched a ride to the line shack, but the driver swore he hadn't seen Sonny since he'd dropped him off.

On foot, they wouldn't have had time to reach the highway before the roadblock went up, so it was a safe bet they were still on the mountain. Sheriff's deputies from three counties fanned out to search isolated houses within a ten-mile radius. As two State Police choppers whirled overhead, Mora County's mounted patrol began to scour the mountainside.

Eighty minutes after the deputy's call, "Officer down!", an unmarked truck with a government plate pulled up in front of the lineshack. A man in a tan uniform with an oakleaf cluster on each shoulder got out. When he opened the back of the truck, a woeful-looking bloodhound tumbled out and relieved himself on the right rear tire.

Rick gave the major Ordell Koonz' black jacket. The major offered it to the dog, and the dog set off at a steady lope, followed by his handler, Rick, and a couple of Santa Fe County sheriff's deputies, George Jaramillo and Gus Ramírez.

The trail led up the mountain, hard going even for somebody in good shape. Gus resolved to cut out desserts in the future. Except his mom's apple pie. Nobody could *not* eat his mom's apple pie. If the serpent had tempted Adam and Eve with Gus' mom's apple pie, God himself would have fallen into sin.

Pearl Partch's wounds were superficial. As the doctor at Northeast Regional tended him, Partch whimpered like a puppy. "I never knowed they wuz goin' kill nobody! You cain't blame me! I never done nothin'," he babbled to the Las Vegas Police Department sergeant guarding him.

"Where's Koonz?" the sergeant demanded.

"I don' know. I'm tellin' y'. I don' know."

"You must know somethin', Pearl. Sure go a lot easier on you if you do."

"Easy! Whaddaya mean?"

"You're accessory to murder. Angel Serrano's dead. Him and his fiancee got a little girl, just three months old. Becky's over there at the funeral home, cryin' her eyes out. And Trini Gabaldón, he's just hanging on. Dunno he's gonna make it." The sergeant shook his head. "Folks is pissed. They come storming in here, I'm just one man. I can't hold 'em off forever."

Pearl blinked. So did the doctor.

"You gotta pertec' me!" Pearl hollered. "I din't shoot nobody!"

"You know, I always liked history in school," the sergeant said. "Always made straight A's. There's a lot of history right here in Las Vegas. You'd be surprised. Most people don't know it, but that hanging tree we got on the plaza…"

Pearl croaked like an amorous frog.

"Folks'll tell you that hanging tree ain't just history. There's sometimes it's used even now. 'Course you never see nothing about it in the *Optic*. Ain't something you'd want everybody to know about. Judges get a little riled sometimes, folks take the law in their own hands."

"You cain't do that! You cain't…"

"Try me," the sergeant said. He smiled.

Pearl croaked some more. Then he told the sergeant everything he knew. He told him about Matty's kidnapping, about the coming millennium and how Erlene's lawsuit was to finance it. He told him about Jaime's threats on Mingo's life, and he confirmed Matty's suspicion that Gordo Gonzáles was involved with Harley Jenks in drug trafficking. But he couldn't shed any light on why Jenks would order Gordo killed.

When he had finished, the sergeant said, "Well, that's just fine. I figger you give us enough to close down your Righteous Sword and

Shield and put you and the preacher away a good long while."

"Wait a minute," Pearl squeaked. "You cain't do that. You cain't! You din't read me my rights. You gotta read me my rights. I watch television. I know the law. It don't count, you don't read me my rights."

All at once, the sergeant was in his face. "You're kinda upset," he said softly. "I read you your rights, only you forgot. Ain't that so, Doc? Tell him. Didn't I read Pearl here his rights?"

The doctor swallowed and slowly nodded his head.

Big Nose Onís was not a happy man. His girlfriend had smuggled a little weed into the South Facility, only the bulls found out about it, and now he was doing T-time in the hole at North while they investigated. What's more, the weed she brought him wasn't very good. Big Nose figured he'd had better highs smoking Chesterfields, only he swore off tobacco when he heard cigarettes cause cancer. Big Nose was scared of the Big C, but he really wanted a cigarette.

What's more, the lieutenant put him in a cell next to Three Legs Thoms. Three Legs wasn't one of Onís' favorite people. He was always a little *loco*, even for an Anglo. But now he was running off at the mouth all the time and wouldn't shut up. Big Nose wanted to stuff a sock in Thoms' mouth or maybe one of them packages, six pairs in assorted colors, like you buy at Walmart.

Captain Torréz came by, making his rounds. Big Nose figured that was one thing to be thankful for. When they transferred the watch commanders in late September, Manny Torréz came on evening watch at the North Facility. Torréz was an okay kind of guy. He wouldn't put up with any crap from anybody: not the inmates, not the administration, and not his officers. Sure, he cut them some slack if he could. Considering the lousy pay, that seemed only reasonable to Big Nose. He had nothing against the bulls. He didn't have anything against the roaches in his cell either, but that didn't mean he wouldn't stomp the suckers if he got the chance.

"Howdy, Onís. *¿Qué pasa?*"

"*Así así.* You know, Captain. Jus' so-so. This ain't no Disneyland in here."

"Is that a fact? Coulda swore I saw Mickey and Goofy walking around the yard this morning arm in arm."

Big Nose laughed. In that moment, he made his decision. Putting his face to the slot in the door, he said quietly, "I gotta talk to you, like now."

Manny nodded, but he didn't say anything.

A couple of hours later, the extraction team came for Onís. He made a big show of protest while they secured him with a belly chain and leg irons. If he was fingered as a snitch, he'd be a dead man, only maybe La EME would protect him. Everybody knew Señor Mustaches wanted Jenks tossed out with the rest of the garbage. Maybe Big Nose could oblige him. Like they say, "There are axes for the tallest pines."

As Big Nose had anticipated, they took him to the captain's office. The captain offered him a smoke, which Big Nose accepted with pleasure.

"So, what's on your mind?" the captain said, doodling on the desk pad in front of him.

Big Nose grinned. "That Thoms, man, he sure got a big mouth."

The captain yawned. Big Nose got the message and settled down to business. "I don't want no write-up, captain. If I gotta get a write-up, lemme do my thirty days in the hole, and lemme go back to population. I don't want to stay up here at the North. Place'll give you the heebie-jeebies."

"You did a bad thing, Onís." The captain shook his head sadly as if Onís were one of his kids scribbling on the walls with a crayon.

"Murder's a more bad thing."

"I'm listening."

So Onís told the captain everything Thoms was saying in the

max: the death of Sweet Papa Foster was a setup. Jenks put Thoms up to it, and Salas gave him the shank.

"*Jenks* did it? Jenks himself and not Salas?"

"The man himself. Guess he wanted to be sure the job got done right. *¿Tienes?*"

"You know what happened to the shank?"

"Sure don't, and that's the God's own truth."

"So, tell me what's in it for Thoms anyhow? Why'd he do something like that even if Warden tells him to?"

"Hell, Thoms' been bitchin' for months he wants to go back to Illinois. He's a in'nerstate transfer. Warden promised him a trip home if he wastes Sweet Papa."

Manny adjusted his glasses. They had an annoying tendency to slip down on his nose. He figured it kept him humble. Big shots don't go around with horn rims on the tips of their noses. "Well, this is all very interesting, Onís, but it don't mean a thing on your say-so, you know? Hearsay testimony."

Big Nose grinned. "Thoms is gettin' awful upset over in Three. Thinks they oughtta shipped him to Joliet right off. Thinks they pulled a fast one on 'im, gettin' 'im to do their dirty work, only they ain't gonna keep their end of it. You talk to 'im, captain. Betcha he'll level with you. Everybody knows you're a real square dude."

Manny sighed. "Yeah, that's what my mother says. Problem is, Onís, no matter what Thoms says, it's just the word of an inmate against the warden."

Big Nose's grin widened. "One inmate, two wardens, and a tape recorder."

Manny sat up with a start.

"Three Legs says warden taped the whole conversation up front so's he could have a hold on Thoms if the dude changes his mind, only maybe he don't never think what's sauce for the goose is sauce for the rooster, you know?"

"The warden offers Thoms a transfer if he kills Foster, and he gets all of this on tape?"

Big Nose nodded.

Manny shook his head in wonder at the follies of mankind. He ordered Big Nose taken back to his cell, but he directed the lieutenant to release him into general population after thirty days. He thought about calling the State Police, but a phone call from the pen on an open line could trigger a fatal accident. Manny didn't want his name on the plaque in Main honoring the memory of valiant officers who had given their lives in the line of duty. Besides, Corrections would probably misspell "Tórrez."

He needed to get a hold of the tape Big Nose was talking about. While he was thinking about that, Rita Martínez walked in. Harley Jenks had asked her to hand deliver the latest revision of the policy governing officers' dress code. *Whole place going to hell in a basket, and Warden's worrying about Windsor knots on a four-in-hand.* Manny asked Rita to sit down. "There's something I want to talk to you about," he said, absentmindedly adjusting his glasses.

Sonny was the Roadrunner outsmarting Wiley Coyote. He knew instinctively the forest canopy would hide the fugitives from the choppers. But, crashing through the brush, he left a trail a pack of Cub Scouts on a Sunday outing could easily follow.

Koonz was breathing hard. He managed to keep up until his chest began to ache from the pain of high altitude exertion. He called a halt to catch his breath.

The preacher sat on a large rock while Sonny danced about him. Something in Sonny's irrepresible energy caused Koonz to snap. He was tired, and he was cold. He'd left his jacket in the line shack. "You stupid fool!"

Sonny came to a stop. "Preacher?"

"Why'd you have to go and shoot 'em? They couldn't do nothin' to us. Wasn't nothin' fer them to find. I seen to that, me and Partch. We took care of everythin'." Koonz' voice was rising as he became more and more agitated.

"Miz Bartle," Sonny said, adjusting the pink bandanna. It had slipped down over one eye. "She tol' me they wuz cops all over the place. She tol' me they got rid of her an' them, and she figgered they wuz goin' to kill you an' Mr. Partch just like King Jesus and John the Baptizer."

"You stupid fool!" Koonz stood up, only to sit down again suddenly. "Almost as dumb as your daddy," he muttered.

"Don't you say that! My daddy is a upright man, judged to be amongst the elect."

Koonz laughed. "Hell, Erlene tol' me she tricked him into marryin' her. Tol' him she was in the family way, and he fell fer it, hook, line, and sinker. Oldest trick in the books."

"They wuz in love!" Sonny insisted.

"She jes' wanted t' get the hell outta that hick town in Missouri and look where he brung her to, Goose Neck, New Mexico. My God! She give 'im two boys, and look what you turned out to be. My God!"

"You shut up!" Sonny cried. "I don't want t' hear you talkin' 'bout my family. Family's important! It's all you ever got. That's why momma's suing the government. 'Cause they took Ikie away from us, and now they gotta pay."

"Listen to you! 'Family's important.' I swear you sound like Danny Quayle." Koonz laughed again. He was beginning to feel lightheaded. "Your momma's suin' 'cause she wants the money. She wants it so's she can give it to me. Old cow thinks she's in love with me." He spat. "She don't give a good goddamn about Ikie, boy, and she sure as hell don't give a damn about you."

In good conscience, Sonny couldn't argue the point, but he insisted, "My daddy, my daddy is a upright man…"

"You tell me, boy, how come he lit out from here and never come back. It's been two years already. You tell me, boy, how come?"

Sonny was about to cry. "I don't know how come. He jes', he jes'…"

"Well, I'm a-gonna tell you, boy," Koonz sneered. 'Cause he never did, that's why. He's buried out under the chicken coop. Come home in the middle of the day, only he found me and yer momma makin' whoopee on the couch. Lord! The way that man lit into her! I hadda brain 'im with the fryin' pan. Yer daddy's gone fer good, boy, only what he left behind is mine, all mine." He leered.

It was too much for Sonny to take in, but one thing Koonz said stuck in his mind like a handprint in wet cement. "My daddy? You kilt my daddy?"

"Like a bug, boy. I squished 'im like a bug." Koonz started up the trail. "C'mon. Let's us git a-goin'."

Sonny raised the Winchester to his shoulder and fired. The bullet hit Koonz in the back. Sonny chambered another round, but the Winchester jammed. He threw it away, as useless to him as every other treasure in his life. Stepping over the prostrate form of the preacher, he scurried away, but he could no longer remember where he was going or why.

Matty was proud of herself. For once, she'd shown good sense. She'd remembered to replace her windshield wiper blades on a bright, sunny day. Her usual philosophy was, if it's sunny, who needs them? And if it's raining, you can't replace them because it's raining and you need them.

She drove the Red Menace to Leyva Automotive. Mr. Leyva'd been dead a few years, but his son-in-law, Monkey García, ran the garage pretty much as the old man had done. Matty'd known Monkey in high school.

"Yo, Monkey, how you doing?"

"Matty Madrid! No shit. How do, *chinita*? Esperanza, she doin' okay?"

"Listen, I need your help. *Mis winshi-waiperos.*"

"Sure thing, sugar."

"Monkey…"

"You still working on that case out at the pen?" Monkey hollered as he rummaged in the back room for a pair of windshield wiper blades. Fred, the garage cat, jumped up on the counter. Matty rubbed the cat's chin, and Fred purred like a finely tuned engine.

"How'd you know about that?"

Monkey poked his head out to say, "This is still a small town, *chinita.* I don't care we got half the state of southern California movin' in. You keep your ear to the ground, you hear things. Here we go!"

She followed him into the parking lot and watched him replace the blades on her *winshi-waiperos.* Sitting in the cab of the truck, Ruggles barked at Fred. The cat regarded the little dog with feline distain.

"Did you know Gordo, Monkey?"

"Him? Hell, no."

"Then…"

"It's my cousin, Freddy. You know Freddy?"

"No, uh-uh, I don't think so."

"Freaky Freddy. He's married to Jeannelle. You see?"

"No…"

"I know all about it 'cause Jeannelle tells Freddy, only Freddy, he tells me. See?"

She shook her head. "I think I lost you on that last curve, Monkey. Jeannelle tells Freddy what?"

"All about the murder." He straightened up. "There you go. Buck fifty, *chinita.*"

"Who the hell is Jeannelle? She work out at the pen or something?"

"Didn't I tell you? Jeannelle Baekke, only before she got married that's who she was. Her brother's Ernie Baekke."

"Two Bits Baekke?"

"Got it in one, *chinita*."

"Monkey, we gotta talk, only don't you call me *chinita*!"

She invited him to join her at McDonald's for a cup of coffee. Ever since the restaurant chain lost a law suit for its too-hot coffee, Matty liked to take her coffee break there. It gave her a warm, cozy feeling, drinking million-dollar coffee.

"Here's the story, doll. Jeannelle got it straight from the horse's ass."

"Mouth. The horse's mouth."

"You ain't met her brother. Anyway, Ernie was, whaddaya call it, shackin' up with Gordo Gonzáles. You know how it goes. Gordo give 'im protection, and Ernie, you know."

"I know." She smiled to herself at Monkey's chivalrous circumlocutions.

"Only Ernie, that *pendejo*, he makes such a ass of himself and gets in a fight with a guard."

"Yeah, I heard."

"Well, they lock him up in solitary so's he'll cool off. See? Only now Gordo's got nobody to whisper sweet somethings into his ear, and Gordo's pissed."

"Go on." So far, Monkey hadn't told her anything she didn't know.

"Gordo goes to the warden. I don't know how come he gets to do that, but he does."

"They were business partners."

"No shit! Ain't that the American way. I'm tellin' you. Anyhow, Gordo tells the warden, you don't let my sweetie outta solitary, I'm gonna blow the whistle on your whole operation. I don't know what Gordo meant by that only maybe you sayin' they was partners an' all, it kinda makes sense."

"Jesus! He threatened to blow the lid off the whole enchilda, so they kill him to shut him up and keep the operation running without a hitch."

"Yeah, but here's the crock," Monkey added. "Gordo never meant to tell nobody nothing. He woulda been incriminating himself, and you can't do that. It's against the law. 'Sides, he don't wanna be fingered as a snitch. He wasn't gonna tell nobody nothing. It was all a bluff."

"And it cost him his life. Jeez! Monkey, what about Two Bits, Ernie? He still in La Pinta?"

"Nah, he got transferred to Southern, so Jeannelle, she don't get to see him no more. She's got a job, you know, and a husband. She can't go runnin' down to Cruces all the time. 'Sides, it ain't like he don't got any friends. Guy like Ernie got lotsa friends, only some of 'em don't know which end is up, is all."

The major from the K-9 Unit looked at his watch and frowned. "Be dark soon," he said. "Better be heading on back."

"Can't your dog track in the dark?"

"He can, but I can't. Too dangerous. Have to use our flashlights, and that makes us a real tempting target. Wind's rising anyway. Be cold tonight."

"Ten more minutes." Gus insisted. "Just ten minutes."

Five minutes later, they found the body of Ordell Koonz. The OMI would say Koonz' life might have been saved had he received prompt medical attention, but all Koonz could do *in extremis* was to scrawl a few letters and numbers into the dirt: ProV3 1 11.

It looked like gibberish to Gus, but Jaramillo, a deacon in the Spanish Pentecostal Church of God in Christ, deciphered the text of the preacher's last sermon. "Proverbs, chapter 31, verse 11: 'The heart of her husband doth safely trust in her, so that he shall have no need of spoil."

Crying his mother's name into the wind, Sonny stumbled through the darkness. From the wilderness of Sonny's soul, there was only one way out.

(HAPTER SEVEN

A bull elk melted into primordial mist. The weather in the high country is as fickle as a woman at a *fandango*. Low-lying clouds caressing the mountaintop whispered the promise of snow. Stowing polar sleeping bags into their packs, the hunters had dressed in multiple layers of wool and cotton. But nobody wants to be stuck on San Antonio Mountain in a blizzard.

At least, Salas was able to get off site for a while. The deputy warden could handle the inmates, and staff was no trouble at all. They were too scared of the Enforcer. But he didn't like outsiders butting in. The interview with Maes stuck in his craw. The sheriff had questioned him about the attempt on that bitch's life. Salas hoped he'd managed to keep his lies sorted out and in order. Like they say, "A liar needs a good memory."

Reese was quiet, which was okay by Salas, only sometimes the brittle silence made him nervous. He felt as if Reese were watching him all the time, processing information like some kind of human computer.

And neither of the hunters had bagged his elk. It was almost as if the animals were extinct, mowed down by a meteor like bowling pins. That's what happened to the dinosaurs a million years ago. He'd read about it in a magazine at the dentist's office.

"Let's hike up the ridge," Reese said. "Take a look around."

At the top of the ridge, Salas paused. A flash of color in the trees below caught his eye, bright red against the gray-green junipers.

Salas saw the flash of the rifle a split second before the bullet hit him, but he never heard the sound of the shot. Falling backwards, he tumbled down the slope until coming to rest against a mound of stones.

Reese watched Marcus Penner emerge from the brush. "You fool!" Reese shouted. "You were supposed to shoot him at point blank range. You were supposed to shoot him with his own gun!"

Penner shrugged. "What's the diff? He's dead, isn't he?"

"The 'diff' is the difference between a Marlin and a Ruger .30-06. Don't you ever think? How do we pass this off as a hunting accident? You were supposed to shoot him with his own gun!"

"Get off my back, will you. You can tell them you never saw the shooter. Tell them it must have been another hunter. Happens all the time."

Reese's eyes flashed. "Salas is wearing a bright orange vest, you idiot. What kind of elk wears a bright orange vest?"

"You get ranchers painting 'COW' on their cattle in whitewash." Penner laughed. "Hunters shoot them anyway. C'mon, let's get out of here."

Reese grudgingly agreed. "We'd better separate. It'll look better that way in case anybody starts to nose around. I'll go for help. Too bad I'm so upset at my friend's death, I'll probably lose my way. Let's hope it doesn't snow for a couple of hours."

Penner grinned. He turned around and headed back the way he had come. An angry David Reese stalked down the mountainside alone.

A magpie alighted on a pole in the middle of the pile of stones where Salas lay. She cocked her head, perplexed. It looked like a dead thing, but keen instincts told her otherwise.

Salas' fingers slowly reached out to the cairn. He gripped a stone at its base so tightly his knuckles whitened.

Startled, the magpie flew away.

Monday morning, Warren Huston, the attorney general's chief criminal investigator, cooled his heels in Reception at the pen's Main Facility. Like Gus, he phoned his boss for instructions. Unlike Gus, Huston did not dial Time and Temperature.

The attorney general promptly placed a call to Warden Jenks. Jenks was in his office, chewing out Carl López. The recreation director could tell him nothing about Gloria Apodaca except she'd submitted her resignation effective immediately. López had no idea where Glo was. Jenks cursed him for his lack of foresight. "You goddam spic! You shoulda knowed the cunt would take a powder. Goddamit!"

Rita buzzed the warden's office.

"Goddamit! I tol' you I wasn't s'pose' to be disturbed!"

"Attorney General Hughes on line one," Rita chirped.

Ninety seconds later, she appeared at Reception to personally escort Warren Huston to the warden's office.

"Mr. Huston!" The warden stuck out a beefy hand. "To what do we owe this pleasure?"

"I don't think it's a pleasure for either one of us." Huston ignored the gesture. "I'm here to investigate allegations of criminal activity."

Jenks smiled a crooked smile. "Well, now. I'm sure we can do that in no time at all. Maybe you'll join me fer lunch when you finish."

"I'm afraid I didn't make myself clear. I'm here to *initiate* an investigation on the orders of the attorney general. You are to give carte blanche to myself and my associates, to the State Police and Assistant Attorney General Salazar. You will authorize the release of any and all documents. You will butt out of any and all witness interrogations. You will make yourself readily available for whatever assistance we require, as will your staff, without exception. Do you understand?"

Jenks could only growl in reply. He ordered Rita to escort the investigator to the South Facility. Huston wanted to see the gym. He intended to impound the equipment, but he didn't tell Jenks that.

On the way over, Rita handed Huston a slip of paper. "It's my phone number," she said, "at home. Anybody asks you, tell 'em you hit on me for a date." A happily married man for thirty-one years, Huston pocketed the slip of paper without any comment.

The blinds of Gloria's duplex were drawn, so Penner figured she was sleeping. Monday was her day off, and he expected her to be in. Since McGuire's death, Gloria never went anywhere as far as he knew. She worked, she shot up, she slept. Sometimes she ate, but not very often.

He banged on the door for ten minutes. Finally, Mr. Moya on the other side stuck his head out to ask what Penner wanted.

"I'm looking for Gloria," Penner explained impatiently.

"She ain't here."

"She go to work today?"

"You don't listen. She ain't here no more."

"What do you mean, old man? Where'd she go?"

"She's gone. Miss Apodaca's moved, and she says to tell you she's leavin' no forwardin' address."

Puzzled, Penner drove to Albuquerque. He dropped by the Kachina Klub to catch rehearsal, but Doomsday Machine was not on stage. The club's manager, five feet of unstable dynamite, came barrelling out of his office when he heard Penner's voice.

"Penner, your band…"

"Hey, Khachigian, where is everybody?"

"Your bass player caught the git-tar player with his pants down.

Unfortunately, your git-tar player was in the girl singer's dressing room at the time. I don't gotta tell you what they was doing. So, the bass player shoots him in the balls with a .45, only your girl singer brains *him* with a lamp. She's in jail until you can make bail, but she's gonna have the bass player for company just as soon's he gets outta the hospital. Just a bump, nothing serious. Now, your git-tar player, he's in University Hospital. He's gonna be okay, but the family jewels… well, he can always audition if you wanna get a new girl singer."

"The drummer…" Penner clung to his last hope.

"He said to tell you 'Chianti' or somethin'. He's gonna go live in a Tibetan lamasery some place. Taos, I think. He said to tell you it's all illusion, and the cricket will devour the frog in the wellspring of time or some crap like that.

"And, by the way," he added, "you owe me for the lamp."

"What lamp?"

"The lamp your singer used to brain your bass player with. $79.99. Call it eighty bucks even. I had 'em made special," the manager said, apparently forgetting he'd bought the lamp on sale at the Price Club for $24.95.

Numbly, Penner reached into his pocket to extract his wallet. The cold steel of handcuffs gripped his wrists.

"Marcus Penner, you're under arrest for trafficking in illicit substances." The detective from the APD recited the familiar warning like a priest pronouncing absolution. "You have the right to remain silent…"

Penner chose to exercise his constitutional rights. He knew the organization rewards a buttoned lip. He also knew what happens to a lip that isn't totally zipped. He'd do time before he'd risk angering the godfather of the Front Range.

Penner was booked into the Bernalillo County Detention Center. The center was so crowded, some twenty inmates were bunking on cots in the day room. When Penner took a look at his new accomodations, he loudly demanded to call an attorney.

"Put a sock in it," one of the inmates said. "I'm tryin' to watch Oprah, dude."

Late Saturday, an alert Forest Service employee spotted Salas' Toyota parked on Forest Route 418. Snow hampered a search of the area by helicopter on Sunday, but on Monday the clouds had lifted, and the chopper spotted what appeared to be the body of a man in the drifts below a hogback ridge. Fortunately, he was wearing a bright orange vest. The chopper radioed Search and Rescue. It took two dozen rescuers five hours in snow and ice to reach the deputy warden and seven more hours to bring him off the mountain.

"He'll live," the weary surgeon at Holy Cross Hospital told the Taos County sheriff's deputy detailed to guard the patient. "Damned if I know why. Sonofabitch must have the constitution of an ox." He shook his head in wonder.

Deputy Calderón, who had barely managed to meet the department's minimum height requirement, grinned. "It's little guys like us live so long, Doc. Wears the big guys down, carrying that heavy frame on you."

The doctor frowned. He could afford to lose a few pounds, but he didn't like to admit it. He went outside to smoke a cigarette.

"Here's what we have so far," the attorney general told the governor. Assistant Attorney General Antonio Salazar sat on the edge of his seat, eager to jump into the conversation. Warren Huston sat stolidly beside him. Like a well-trained child, Huston would speak only when spoken to. At last, the attorney general nodded for him to begin.

"The warden's secretary will testify to incriminating conversations she's overheard. So will the switchboard operator. The recreation officer, Gloria Apodaca, who found the body of Isaac Gonzáles, has stated she was ordered by Deputy Warden Salas to leave her post in the gym shortly before the murder. The lab's going over the weight bench, the bar, and the weights with the proverbial fine tooth comb. Gloria'll also testify the physician's assistant, McGuire, was threatened by the deputy warden. McGuire suspected Gonzáles was murdered. McGuire's death is officially a suicide, but Sheriff Maes is about to reopen the case." Huston never bothered to refer to his notes. He didn't trust documentation and committed to memory everything he had learned.

"A private investigator, Marta Madrid, was hired by the Gonzáles family to gather evidence concerning the supposedly accidental death of Isaac Gonzáles. She believes that Jenks ordered Gonzáles killed to prevent his blowing the whistle on criminal activities at the pen. It appears Jenks and Gonzáles were engaged in a conspiracy to furnish controlled substances to prisoners and smuggling contraband into a correctional institution."

"Both fourth-degree felonies," Salazar interjected.

"This man Partch in Las Vegas confirms it."

"Hearsay." The AAG shook his head. "Did you find Gonzáles' brother and the preacher?"

"Koonz is dead. Sonny Gonzáles seems to have vanished off the face of the earth."

Huston continued his summary. "Marta Madrid also has information linking Jenks and Salas to at least four other killings. Inmate Thoms has given us a statement confirming the taped conversation Captain Tórrez made available in which Jenks persuades him to murder Inmate Foster, who, in turn, was importuned by the warden into murdering Isaac Gonzáles."

"What about this fellow Thoms?" the governor asked. "Why is he so eager to cooperate? Isn't he charged with murder?"

"Prosecuting a lifer on a murder charge isn't worth the bother."

Salazar shrugged. "Besides, we need Thoms' testimony to stick it to Jenks and company."

"Thoms is being sent out of state," Huston added. "He was an interstate transfer anyway. Officially, it's to keep him out of harm's way. Unofficially… well, he should be on his way to Chicago by now." The investigator looked at his watch.

"Should be, but isn't," Salazar said. "When the marshals went to get him, the pen had lost the paperwork."

The governor frowned. "You think that's more evidence of a criminal conspiracy?"

Salazar shook his head. "Just another foul-up. It's typical of Corrections. The marshals are under orders not to leave the pen without him. They're a couple of hard-assed sons-of-bitches. They can wait."

"Speaking of paperwork," Huston continued, "we're slowly ferreting out a lot of supporting documentation in the pen's files."

"Files?"

Huston suppressed a smile. "That's one of the more interesting things about the place. The official motto of Corrections may be 'Firm, fair, and consistent,' but unofficially it's 'Cover your ass.' It looks like every legal and illegal act since 1954 has been memoed or logged or otherwise documented so somebody can claim, 'It's not my fault. They made me do it, and I've got the documentation to prove it.' Hell, the officers even log a 10-64."

"What the hell's that?"

"A potty break."

Salazar snorted. Huston allowed himself to smile.

The governor didn't seem to think it was funny. "You're telling me you've got enough to nail Jenks and his cronies?"

"To the wall. With the testimony of Thoms, Guy, and Salas…"

"Salas?"

"He can't stop talking. Ever since he came to, Salas has been squawking like a parrot on speed. Jenks tried a little too hard to tie up loose ends, and Salas is going to be the noose around his neck. "

"You'd better mount a guard on his hospital room," Salazar said.

"Done."

"What about Reese?" the governor asked.

Anson Hughes shook his head. "All we've got on Reese is unsupported testimony from Salas and Rita Martínez. If Salas cops a plea, a clever defense attorney can easily call his testimony into question as tainted. The conversation Rita overheard is a little ambiguous. And, unlike Jenks, Reese is too shrewd to leave a paper trail. We'll wait to take him down another day."

"Gurulé?"

"Gilbert Gurulé is too dumb to know his ass from asbestos. No, he's clean."

"Good." The governor nodded decisively. It was a gesture which had served him well in a televisual age. "I'll tell Gilbert to put Jenks on administrative leave pending a full investigation. Soon's you get an indictment, I'll fire the SOB. It's not like he was a native anyway."

"Poor New Mexico," Salazar said unexpectedly. "So far from God and so close to Texas."

The governor didn't seem to hear him. He was too busy chewing over the information he'd been forcefed by the AG's office. There was a lot of gristle in it, and he found it hard to swallow.

Jenks would have to go, the governor decided, Jenks and Salas. Give the deputy warden a break in exchange for his testimony so they could nail the warden's hide to the barn door. Gurulé would stay in the administration until after the election, then he'd find something else for Gilbert to do. Maybe he could help the first lady with one of her little projects.

The governor was a political realist. He was also a fair-to-middling poker player, who knew when to fold.

Sometime Thursday, David Reese stumbled upon a Game and Fish officer on the west face of the mountain. Attempting to lend verisimilitude to his story, Reese had wandered off the trail only to lose his way. He'd spent the last four nights in a snow cave above the tree line before venturing out into the sunshine.

"My friend! My friend's hurt." His voice was raspy. "You've got to help him. He's been shot!"

The officer radioed base. Grinning, he said, "Man, have I got good news for you. Brought your friend out a couple days ago. He's at Holy Cross, but it looks like he's going to make it." The officer, a native of Taos pueblo, didn't mention Salas had been found clinging to the base of a shrine sacred to the pueblo. Some people'd say it was just a coincidence, and maybe that's all it was.

Reese sneezed. He'd caught a chill on the mountain. "Get me to a telephone," he rasped.

Under orders from the Department of Public Safety, Corporal Ulibarri, the biggest man in the Taos Police Department, kept watch outside Salas' hospital room.

"Officer, you've got a call downstairs."

"Downstairs? Hey, Doc. How come they didn't call me on the radio?"

The doctor shrugged. Ulibarri headed down the hall towards the elevator. The doctor looked around him before slipping into the dimly lit room. He gingerly removed a pillow from under Salas' head and covered the deputy warden's face.

"I wouldn't do that if I was you."

The doctor spun around. Deputy Calderón was pointing his weapon at a vital portion of the doc's anatomy.

"Get the fucking *culo*," Salas screamed from the bed.

The doctor threw the pillow at the deputy and ran to the open door, but it was blocked by the massive shape of Corporal Ulibarri.

The deputy put his hand on the doctor's shoulder. "Shandler, Shandler, Shandler. Outta the joint two months and you in trouble already." He clucked his tongue.

"You can't pin this on me," Shandler squeaked. "I never laid a hand on him."

"What you talkin' 'bout?" Calderón said. "We got you for impersonatin' a doctor. Ain't that right, Ulibarri?"

Corporal Ulibarri laughed merrily.

When Matty approached the CO in the lobby at the South Facility, she was surprised to see her shake her head. "No visitors. The joint's in lock-down."

"How come?" Matty asked. "What's going on?"

The CO shrugged. "Beats me," she said. "They never tell me nothing. They could open the sally port and let them all out and I'd never know."

Matty wasn't about to waste her time strolling through the bushes, as the saying goes, even though she'd hoped to talk to Mingo. Maybe he could fill in some of the blanks, but that would have to wait.

As she walked through the parking lot, a white Isuzu pulled in. She was surprised to see Manny Tórrez at the wheel. It was after 2:00, evening watch, and Manny should be at his post at the North Facility. She wondered what he was doing at the South.

Manny introduced her to Assistant Attorney General Salazar. She'd already met the third member of the party, Warren Huston. The investigator had interviewed her in depth. He'd asked to see her notes on the case, but she'd told him some of her information was confidential. "I don't intend to let anybody read it. You understand?"

"I could get a court order, compel you to turn over your notes."

"You do that, and I'll eat them." Huston hadn't pressed the point. He pegged Matty as a woman of her word. If the salsa's hot enough, you can eat anything.

"What's happening?" she asked. "How come the joint's in lockdown?"

"I'm afraid that's my fault," Salazar said. "We've reviewed all the documents in the case…"

"The ones we had access to," Huston said pointedly.

"We've been talking to staff," the AAG continued, "and we're about to question inmates. It seemed simpler if we could do so without impeding inmate accountability."

"Seems to me they're in here because they think they're not accountable to anybody."

"No, I mean their presence in class, at the library, on the job. That's what's meant by 'inmate accountability.' Instead of sorting out who's where, we leave them in the housing units where we can find them."

"Besides," Matty added with a smile, "sometimes security can't even find them unless they're in lockdown." She'd been in Visits when the visiting officer spent precious minutes trying to track down an inmate. "Try the library," the unit officer would suggest. "Maybe he's in the yard. You try foot patrol?" The pen's inmate accountability system wouldn't exactly inspire the public's confidence if the public only knew. Maybe he's escaped and he's terrorizing the community. Or maybe he's in the gym, mashing the brains of Gordo Gonzáles.

"Their attorneys ain't gonna be too happy 'bout that," Manny said. "Visits, Education, Library—the whole shebang is under court order."

"I'm well aware of that, Captain. My boss, Anson Hughes, is meeting in judge's chambers this afternoon, hoping to persuade his honor a full-scale investigation of murder and corruption takes precedence over the letter of the law.

"In the meantime, Ms. Madrid, I've reviewed the files, and I'd really like to talk to you. That is, if you have the time."

Matty nodded. To her surprise, she was ushered into the South Facility through the double doors, bypassing the metal detector. Salazar preempted the associate warden's office for their interview. He closed the door in the associate warden's face and locked it.

The interview itself was unremarkable. Matty explained how she happened to be on the case and what she'd learned, including creative financing at the Church of the Righteous Sword and Shield. Matty praised Leroy Maes and his deputies for their hard work. That ought to make up for all those free cups of coffee she'd cadged from the sheriff's office.

After the interview ended, Matty stopped at Allsup's to buy ten dollars worth of unleaded at $1.33 a gallon. "Damn," she said aloud. She should have asked the AAG how come gas is so high in New Mexico, especially in Santa Fe. Tony Abeyta told her it was lots cheaper in Austin. Every so often, a state legislator or somebody in the AG's office promises an investigation, but nothing ever comes of it. Maybe they're all driving state cars and using state-owned credit cards. It's the poor slob who pays the bills every month feels the pinch.

She wasn't really serious. She wouldn't discuss price-fixing with Salazar, but thinking about it put an idea into her head. She wondered if the AAG knew what Mrs. Gonzáles meant when she said, "They was all afraid of Ikey. They knowed he *wuz on the payroll.*"

She drove back to the pen. At the entrance on Highway 14, the traffic barrier was up, and no CO was at the post. Matty looked at the clock on the dash. 4:15. The joint would ordinarily be in lockdown for count anyway, and all visitors sent packing. The teachers, the nurses, and the PA's would be at Rodeo Nites, trying frantically to unwind, never realizing if you unwind a spring too often, it's sprung.

As Matty drove past the warehouse, she was struck by the eerie solitude of an institution in lockdown. She was used to seeing staffers going in and out of the training annex, visitors cruising along the roads, minimums swapping stories with PPS outside the garage or depleting the aquifer to water the warden's roses. Eleven hundred people live in La Pinta, but it seemed like a ghost town.

Approaching the South Facility, Matty figured the tower would spot her. He'd radio perimeter patrol to check her out. Perimeter patrol drives in circles around the facility like a wind-up toy, only wind-up toys don't carry loaded rifles.

All of a sudden, Matty saw a man running towards the sally port. He was wearing greens: an inmate. She felt a prickle of fear on the back of her neck, and she stopped the truck in the middle of the roadway. No inmate is allowed outside his cell during count unless he's on an outcount. There'd have to be a good reason for an outcount. Say, if he was unloading a truck.

But there was no truck.

On an impulse, Matty turned left and drove to the sally port which consisted of two sets of gates, an inner one and an outer one. A delivery truck, the chow truck, say, passes through the outer gate. The inner gate opens only after the outer gate is secured. Because both gates are not open at the same time, no inmate can escape in a mad dash to freedom.

There was still no sign of the perimeter patrol.

Matty left her truck and quickly strode over to the sally port. She lost sight of the running man until he turned a corner and came into plain view.

Mingo.

He didn't see her. She wanted to call out to him, but his name died on her lips.

"¡*Cuidado,* bro!"

She heard a voice from somewhere overhead, but it didn't sound like the voice of God unless you believe God speaks Spanglish. The housing units were less than ten years old, but the walls were already cracking. Mingo told her some of the cells were so exposed to the elements they had become uninhabitable. She could see a man's face peering through a foot-wide crack on the second floor. She recognized Jaime Gonzáles.

"*¡Cuidado!*" Jaime shouted again. "Look out, bro! Behind you!"

Mingo crouched behind a pile of empty boxes by the sally port. Several yards away, Warden Jenks waved what looked like a Smith & Wesson in one hand and a radio in the other. He barked commands into the radio. "10-72. *All* personnel ordered to secure. Repeat: 10-72." Amid the ruins of his crumbling empire, nobody would see Harley Jenks destroy the one man who, by his own calculation, had brought him down, Mingo.

If the goddam spic hadn't never brung his girl friend into it. If he'd jes' kept his mouth shut. Why couldn't the sonofabitch keep his mouth shut? Don't they never learn! Gordo wasn't nothin' to him. He wasn't like Baekke. He didn't have the hots for him or nothin'.

In the tower, Sergeant Bowles was so intent on the drama unfolding beneath him he failed to see Matty at all. Bowles clutched his rifle nervously, waiting for the warden to give him the command to lock and load.

Gurulé says, "You go on ad leave." Hell, the last warden they put on ad leave got canned. He thinks I don't know what's goin' on. Dammit, I didn't jes' fall offa no turnip truck. Goddammit!

Jenks was puffing like a tea kettle. He was overweight, and his only regular exercise was walking from the couch to the refrigerator. Mingo was half his age, and Mingo kept in shape. Just like Gordo, Mingo kept in shape by working out.

Working out. Working out on that damned bench in the goddam gym. It don't matter. There's only so many places Mínguez can run, jes' so many places he can hide. He can't run forever. Nobody runs forever.

Matty dashed back to the Toyota. Fumbling in the glove compartment, she took out the Browning, and checked to see if it was loaded. From behind the gate of the sally port, she watched the deadly game of cat and mouse.

"Get down!" Mingo had spotted her.

Jenks saw her, too. "Tower! 10-80. Waste her!"

"What?"

"You heard me! Waste the goddam cunt! Shoot the spic, too."

"You never told me to 'Lock and load,'" Bowles wailed.

"Oh, fer… lock and load, you son of a whore!"

Matty had a split second in which to decide. She could try to take out Jenks, but he was hiding in the shadow of a trash container, waiting for Mingo to make his move. While she was aiming at the warden, the tower would have her in his sights.

Or she could shoot the officer in the tower, giving Jenks open season on Mingo. Besides, the tower was probably beyond the Browning's range.

Bowles made her mind up for her. His first shot missed her by a country mile, but his second sprayed gravel at her feet.

She steadied her arm and took aim. She tried to imagine herself on the midway at the State Fair, shooting little yellow ducks in a row to win a big blue teddy bear. She fired. Bowles catapulted out of the tower, landing with a thud on the roof of the hobby shop.

Matty heard a scream. It sliced through her heart like a knife through a boiled potato. *¡Jita!* For a split second, she thought it was Bowles. It couldn't be Mingo. It had to be Bowles. But the scream didn't come from the roof. *¡Esperanza!* The scream came from the direction of the sally port.

"Mingo?"

Mingo stood in the yard, gulping air like a drowning man. Harley Jenks lay dead at his feet, a knife in the middle of his back.

A black man in greens crept out of the shadows. He squatted beside Jenks and poked the warden to see if he was really dead.

"Washington," Mingo said. His voice cracked. "Lamar… you saved my life."

"Chill out, man. You don' count for beans. Mah ace, Sweet Papa, mah ace, he can sleep now. Ah done paid in full all he owed an' den some."

"The shank…"

The ghost of a smile played on Washington's lips. "Shit, man, dat's d' shank dem double clutchers use' to kill 'im wit'. Dat's d' shank, man. Spidey pick it up in d' yard when Foster cash it in. He give it t' me, an' I hid it in d' horseshoe pitch where de Man ain't ever goin' find it.

"He don' show mah ace no respect, man. Now he daid. T'ree daid men in d' yard, man, Jenks and Bowles…"

"Washington…"

"An' dat's d' other one." He sighed. "Ah'm a daid man, Mínguez. All dat's left is dem t' bury me."

Trini Gabaldón woke in intensive care at Northeast Regional. He had no idea where he was or how he'd gotten there. The first thing he saw was his wife's face. He wondered why she looked so worried. Maybe she'd forgotten to make the payments on little Rudy's bike.

"Mary Anne?"

"Trini! I'm here, sweetheart."

"Mary Anne, you gotta make the payments, only tell Corrine a Maytag." He closed his eyes. "It lasts and lasts." Sleep called him like a lover to her bed.

"Doctor?" Mary Anne Gabaldón was afraid her husband was slipping away, talking funny. It's like that sometimes before the end. Her mother's brother got up and dressed to go to work, and him retired from the railroad sixteen years.

The doctor patted her on the shoulder. "He's going to be all right, Mrs. Gabaldón. Don't you worry."

"A twenty-four-inch," Trini mumbled, "with a handbrake." Maytags don't have handbrakes, but he couldn't think. Thinking was like swimming in oatmeal. Trini fell asleep, dreaming of Bridge Street. He was six years old, riding a brand-new second-hand bike down Bridge Street. His father ran beside him, holding the bike steady.

You can do it, Trinidad! Hang on, son. Hang on!

His dad let go, but Trini didn't stop. *Watch me, Daddy. Watch me!*
All the way down Bridge Street, the child Trini was at one with the
wind and the song of the river.

Tommy Varela was only ten, but his father could hardly contain
his pride in his son. He thought it would bubble out of him like car-
bonated soda. Watching Tommy grow to manhood was Ben's chief
joy. Surely, the Holy Family must have felt this way about the child
Jesús. The Blessed Mother and San José knew to embrace a child is to
hold the world in your arms.

Like Ben, San José was a father and a woodworker. The saint
had known the smell of green wood, the pressure of an adze on
calloused hands.

Ben Varela earned his living as a wood cutter and *santero*. By
mid-November, he could count several cords of wood stacked beside
his house in Rowe. Six days a week, Thanksgiving through Easter,
Ben drove his pickup to Santa Fe and parked at the intersection of
Old Pecos Trail and the Old Las Vegas Highway, where vendors peddle
chile ristras, pumpkins, and apples in autumn. In winter, woodcutters
sell Christmas trees and piñon wood to the *villeros*.

On Sundays, after mass, after Lucy had cleared away the breakfast dishes, Ben sat down at the kitchen table. Sometimes Tommy sat
beside him to do his homework. Ben helped him memorize his times
tables or the capitals of all fifty states. And all the while, Ben's hands
worked to free from the pine the body of a saint.

Long ago, when the only source of trade to New Mexico was a
caravan which trundled up El Camino Real from Chihuahua every
other year, New Mexicans had learned to do for themselves. *Santeros,*
saint makers, untutored and unknown, carved numinous statues of
Cristo, the Most Holy Trinity, the Blessed Virgin, Antonio, Ysidro La-

brador, Santiago, Juan Nepomuceno, and all the blessed company of saints. But the coming of the Americans and increased trade with the eastern seaboard made cheap plaster saints readily available. The art of the *santero* was dying until it was revived as "folk art" and given a new cachet.

Ben Varela didn't put much faith in fashion, but he figured it hardly mattered whether he carved a *santo* for an altarpiece or a *nicho* in somebody's living room. When Ben carved, when he watched Lucy paint the bare wood in bright reds, blues, and yellows, he knew their hands grasped the hand of God, the Master Worker, Who crafted all the saints of Paradise in His own image.

Saturday morning, Lucy packed a lunch, and the three of them drove along an old Forest Service road into the mountains. Ben's ancestors had cut wood in what is now the Santa Fe National Forest for generations. Like his forefathers, Ben seldom cut down a living tree. By harvesting a single limb on this tree and another one on that, in the old way, he insured the future of the forest. The tree would continue to grow, to supply more wood another year, another generation, as a rose bush blossoms every summer.

While Ben and Lucy finished their tamales, Tommy wandered to the rim of a narrow canyon a few yards away. Be careful! The words formed themselves in Ben's head, trying to work their way into his larynx and onto his tongue, but he swallowed them whole. He's a big boy, he told himself. He don't need you clucking over him like a wet hen. He glanced at Lucy. She watched Tommy as an eagle watches its fledgling's first attempt to fly.

"Dad!" Ben's heart stopped. "Dad! Come over here. Look!"

Three hundred feet down was the body of a man. For a moment, Ben's eyes focused on a small ledge where a creosote bush clung tenaciously. He didn't want to look at the broken body on the canyon floor. Strange the creosote bush could live in such an unlikely place and a man should die. Wrapped in a pink bandanna, the man's head lay at an odd angle to his torso. Ben knew the man was dead, his neck broken. He must have jumped off the cliff or maybe he fell in the dark of night. Ben couldn't think of any reason for somebody to run through the woods by moonlight. Maybe he was a witch. Ben shook his head. A witch would have flown to safety on the tawny wings of an owl.

Lucy fell to her knees in prayer. That roused Ben to say, "C'mon, girl. We gotta tell the sheriff." The mountain was crawling with cops early in the week. Maybe this was the man they'd been looking for. Some fella shot Sheriff Gabaldón. But it didn't matter who he was. You don't leave a Christian soul in the mountains to lie unburied like carrion, a feast for the crows. Ben hoped the coyotes wouldn't find the body before he could bring help. He'd heard them howling last night, the dogs of God, their plaintive song older than time itself. The moon could fall into the sea and the sun burn out like a candle stub, but coyotes would howl into the darkness like the voices of the damned.

Saturday night, Matty joined Rodney and Dodi at Dappertuto's for a drink. "Yo, Rod, what's happening?" she demanded.

Rodney sipped his J & B. "Jenks' death effectively cancels out the awesome potential for scandal, more's the pity. Salas, of course, will be prosecuted for attempted murder, yours, my sweet, on the basis of Artful Guy's decidedly artless testimony, not to mention the money in departmental funds which ended up in Guy's bank account. There's not enough evidence to support a murder case, absenting eye-witness testimony."

"Buckets!"

"That is to say, reliable eyewitness testimony. Besides, you told me Salazar doesn't know about, uh, Buckets. Remember? But drug charges might, *might*, stick."

"Like rubber cement."

"Hmmm? Actually, I rather suspect the DA will allow Salas to cop a plea. The man is a veritable fount of information to rival the Encyclopaedia Britannica. And a guilty plea would avoid the scandal of a trial, so the governor's likely to apprise the attorney general of his wishes in that respect. Your friend Sergeant Bowles, how embarrassing to be so startled by gunfire one tumbles out of a tower and onto a workshop, breaking one's leg into the bargain. Tsk, tsk, tsk. He'll be a guest of the state for quite some time as soon as he gets out of the hospital."

"Matty didn't shoot him?"

"At that range? And with a Tennyson?"

"Browning," Matty said, laughing. "You got Tennyson on the brain. What about David Reese?"

"Not enough to indict, but he'll certainly be treading on thin ice, skating on eggshells—whatever. Shandler's statement raises a number of interesting possibilities. Shandler is the sinew…"

"The muscle."

"…Reese purportedly hired to subtract Salas from the equation after Penner failed to do so. Incidentally, the bullet that almost killed Salas came from Penner's rifle. Tacky! But, lack-a-day, there's no hard evidence to support the allegation that Reese was behind the, um, hits. And Penner's too good a fella to squeal, as it were, on the mob. But the authorities are reexamining the deaths of Francis McGuire, Pauley Gallegos, and Herbert Karr. Karr was a numbers runner, by the by. The organization's going to be less than overjoyed with Penner if he did, indeed, have Karr murdered by means of an injudicious overdose.

"Reese, I'm sorry to say, somehow failed to keep receipts for his contract killings. I don't suppose they're deductible anyway. At the moment, he's in a hospital in Taos, recuperating from a nasty bout with pneumonia. Hunting for deputy wardens in a snowstorm is decidedly not recommended for one's health."

"Secretary Gurulé? What about him?"

Rodney smiled. "Haven't you heard? The feds tapped him to head the new facility in Colorado. The governor is, no doubt, heaving an enormous sigh of unmitigated relief."

"Gurulé? *¡Oh, chiste!*"

"High profile appointment for a Spanish-surnamed individual. Brownie points all around."

"Shit! We got *pendejos*, too, just like anybody. It's a free country. This is *loco*, Rod. The whole department needs a shakeup. The public…"

Rodney patted her hand. "Ducky-bumps, let it go. The public doesn't care about the pen so long as inmates politely refrain from pillaging the countryside. More to the point, the governor told me to tell you through the agency of Antonio Salazar that you won't be prosecuted on a weapons charge if you do but keep your ruby lips sealed. Bringing weapons into a correctional institution is a definite no-no, you know."

"Yeah, well, I didn't actually take it into the facility. I was outside of the fence the whole time."

Rodney smiled. "Don't fret, pet," he said. "The system will, in time, digest its problems."

"Yeah, like bacteria in a cesspool, growing fat and sassy on the shit they devour. Speaking of shit, Manny Tórrez tells me the Denver mob is out on its ear, drugwise, at the pen."

"Good news!" Dodi said.

"Kinda. Left a vacuum. The Mexican mafia moved right in, only the *sindicato's* into meth 'stead of H. More profitable, maybe a 600 percent return on your initial investment. You can change wardens or whatever, but the drug trade goes right on."

"Supply and demand."

She shook her head. "Until we get a governor who's determined to reform the joint and not just paying lip service to what the court decrees, the place'll be a cesspool all right."

"Speaking of which," Rodney said, "who's the new warden? I suppose Corrections will yet again resort to bringing in hired guns from out of state."

"Not this time. At least, not yet. The acting warden is former Captain Manuel Tórrez."

Everybody grinned.

"Matty, I don't understand one thing." Dodi frowned. "How did Mingo and the other guy, Washington, how'd they get out? You said the place was locked down…"

"Jenks ordered everybody to stay put, but he told the unit officer to let Mingo out so he could kill him. He wanted to waste him himself. I guess he didn't trust his stooges anymore. They'd made such a godawful mess of everything else."

"And Washington?"

"Washington was just waiting for an opportunity to get to Jenks or Salas. He wanted revenge for his friend, Foster. When they called Quarters shortly after chow, he knew something was up, so he took a chance one of the wardens would come into the yard. He didn't know the assistant AG had called the lockdown. In fact, Salazar was interviewing inmates in their housing units at about that time. If Jenks hadn't been so single-minded about killing Mingo, he wouldn't have been there, and he'd probably be alive today."

"So, Washington didn't report back to his cell, his housing unit?"

"He left the library like everybody else, only he made a little detour and hid in the trash container by the sally port. If any inmates saw him there, they didn't say anything. Surprise, surprise."

"And the guards didn't even miss him?"

"Oh, yeah. The unit officer was on the ball and reported him missing to the lieutenant, but Jenks couldn't think about anything except whacking Mingo. He told the lieutenant to can it till later, only later never came."

"I'll bet that all went into the officer's log."

"You bet it did. Anyhow, I guess Washington's fate's in the hands of the Public Defender's office now."

Rodney cleared his throat. "Actually, Kleiner, Sprague and Stone does a modicum of *pro bono* work now and again, so I thought…"

"Oh, Rodney!" Dodi said, amazed. "You're going to represent Lamar Washington! Sonofagun!"

"Dodi," Matty asked, "how does it stand with the lawsuit?"

Dodi shook her head. "Mrs. Gonzáles won't return any of my calls. The guy in the bar, he's a cousin or something, he says she just wanted the money for Ordell Koonz. So, with him out of the picture…"

"Gotcha. And with Sonny dead…"

"The good news is the sheriff Sonny shot is going to be all right. He regained consciousness this morning. But the guy, Max, he said Mrs. Gonzáles hardly seems to care. Just sits in her living room, staring at the TV. You know, the funny thing is, under the circumstances, I could probably negotiate a settlement for Mrs. Gonzáles, if she'd just okay it."

"I hope so," Matty said. "Otherwise, you and me are gonna be out a lot of work with nothing to show for it." She wondered if it was worth thirty-three cents to bill Erlene for the knit skirt. At least she had Al Montana's $75 plus his $250. But she didn't have Dodi's retainer yet. "Dodi…"

"Actually," Dodi said with a grin, "don't be too sure about that. About having nothing to show for it, I mean. I've been asked to file a wrongful death suit in connection with this case, Matty, and I could use your help. Win or lose, it's bound to get me, us, a lot of attention. And you know there's really no such thing as bad publicity."

Rodney looked up from his drink. "Wrongful death, Dod? Whose? Jenks?"

She shook her head.

"Foster?" Matty asked. "Gallegos? McGuire? Angel Serrano?"

"No, no, no, and no." Dodi was grinning broadly. "My client is a woman named Amber Plank. She lives in Evergreen, Washington. She's divorced and has two kids."

"Who?"

"Amber Bissel Plank, Lucius Bissel's sister. She's suing for wrongful death *and* a 1983. The wrongful death claim will probably be dismissed, but what the hell. I think we have a case under the Eighth Amendment. If the death penalty's not cruel and unusual punishment, I don't know what is." Matty made a face. "Somebody, the Coalition to Stop Senseless Violence I think it's called, paid a retainer on Mrs. Plank's behalf. They're prepared to take this all the way to the Supreme Court, and so am I."

"The U.S. Supreme Court?"

Dodi grinned like a Cheshire cheese, as Cipi would say. "And, anyhow, I got back the assets Herbie stole. So, I'll pay you just as soon as I get your bill."

They ordered another round of drinks. It was Matty's turn to pay, so she took a five and a couple of ones out of her wallet. Two pieces of cardboard fell into her lap. She excused herself to use the telephone.

"Zeke? Hiya, Zeke. It's Matty. *¡Así así!* Listen, I was thinking, I got two tickets to the circus tomorrow, and maybe... Okay, I'll see you then. 2:00 PM. Should be a barrel of laughs. Yeah, barrels of monkeys, too. I promise. *¡Bueno,* bye!"

She hung up, smiling to herself. Life's a circus, only we can't all be starring in the center ring. Somebody's gotta sweep up after the elephants.

Thank you, Christina Alvarez, Jane Dystel,
Vicki Goldberg, Barbara Gordon,
Penny Harter, Susan Hazen-Hammond,
Melanie Kershaw, Sarah Lovett,
Debbie Notkin, Judy Rossner,
Tamar Stieber, Peggy van Hulsteyn,
and Cynthia Webb -- a baker's dozen of readers,
writers, and all-around good people.